E. Mason

Ventriloquism Made Easy

also, an exposure of magic, and the second sight mystery

E. Mason

Ventriloquism Made Easy
also, an exposure of magic, and the second sight mystery

ISBN/EAN: 9783337390082

Printed in Europe, USA, Canada, Australia, Japan

Cover: Foto ©Andreas Hilbeck / pixelio.de

More available books at **www.hansebooks.com**

VENTRILOQUISM MADE EASY,

ALSO, AN EXPOSURE OF

AND THE

SECOND SIGHT MYSTERY,

By E. MASON, Jr.
(OUR NED.)

———— ✦ ————

All things being are in mystery: we expound mysteries by mysteries;
And yet the secret of them all is one in simple grandeur:
All intricate, yet each path plain, to those who know the way;
All unapproachable, yet easy of access, to them that hold the key.

———— ✦ ————

PHILADELPHIA:
WYMAN THE WIZARD, PUBLISHER.
C. E. P. BRINCKLŒ & CO., PRINTERS, No. 23 NORTH SIXTH STREET.
1 8 6 0.

Ventriloquism Made Easy, &c.

Description of the Magician's Table,
AS USED BY EVERY PROFESSOR OF MAGIC.

THE following cut gives a correct view of a magician's table; and exhibits to the reader a ready explanation of many of their best tricks, manner of execution, etc. These tables are, however, dispensed with by many of the most skilful magicians, and dexterity of movement is now more relied upon than mechanical contrivance. Professor Robert Houdon, of Paris; William Feikle, the Russian magician, now creating a great excitement in London; and Professor Wyman, who is never behind the age in improvements in his art, have entirely dispensed with the use of the table.

When a secret confederate is required, have a table four and a half feet long, two feet eight inches high, two feet nine inches wide, with a curtain round it, twenty-two inches deep. In the top of this table are several secret square holes, of different sizes, from three to five inches across; these having covers which exactly fit, and hung upon concealed hinges, so that they may be let down; but when lying flat, the top of the table appears to present a perfect surface. Under this surface are buttons, which prevent those lids from falling down when not made use of. Under the top

3

of the table is fastened a box, or drawer, open at the top, and at the side which is farthest from the specta-tors. This box is about twenty inches deep, and con-cealed by the curtain ; and into this box is placed the secret agent, who assists the performer.

McAllister's Great Trick.
CUTTING OFF THE NOSE.

McALLISTER was a Scotchman by birth,—a man of superior abilities and great mechanical genius. His name stood high as a magician in Spain, France, and Portugal ; and in the United States he commanded a position in the front rank as a performer, as well as a gentleman and scholar. With Americans he was always very popular, drawing large houses in every place where he gave his really excellent entertainments. McAllister died in Keokuk, Iowa, a few years since, lamented by many warm admirers and devoted friends. His professional success in life is, doubtless, to be attributed to his easy manner, graceful deportment, and gentlemanly address, and the skill of his manager.

This feat, though it has a very horrifying appearance, need cause no alarm, as it is one of the simplest tricks which can be attempted. The performer ought to be a short distance from the company when it is to be performed, and must be provided with two clasp-knives, one of which must have a small semi-circle cut out of it—the other being a common knife ; of course you show the latter to the company as the only instrument in your possession ; you must also provide yourself with a small piece of sponge soaked in wine, and, having caused an individual to sit down, you immediately proceed to work, by slipping the true knife into your pocket, and producing the other in its place ; then put your left hand, with the sponge in it, upon the person's brow, and pass the knife gently over his nose, so that the semi-circle which is in the knife will cause it to descend, and, to all appearance, cut into his nose, while you squeeze the sponge gently, so that it may appear to bleed.

To Pour Wine, Vinegar, and Water out of the Same Bottle.

PROFESSOR ANDERSON'S TRICK.

PROFESSOR JOHN H. ANDERSON, the Wizard of the North, has the most extensive reputation, as a magician, of any person living, having performed before all the crowned heads of Europe, and also in all the principal cities of the United States to crowded houses. He is very pleasing in his address, and unequalled in the manner of performing his feats. He is a Scotchman by birth, and now giving his pleasing entertainments in the United States. Professor Anderson has probably made more money in this country than any other performer in the profession.

This little experiment will occasion contradiction with some, and amusement to all.

Provide a common black junk bottle, with rather a large opening at the mouth ; have three tin tubes the same height as the bottle, inside, with three holes at the sides near the end of each tube, which you introduce into three small bladders; the openings being tied two-thirds of the distance of the length of the tubes from the bottom. The bladders with the tubes are now placed in the bottle ; fill them, separately, with wine, vinegar, and water ; the water and vinegar being colored the same as the wine. These tubes can be fastened in the neck of the bottle with cork, and come up even with the mouth of the bottle. If you wish to pour out wine, take the bottle by the neck with your hand, placing your thumb over the other two holes of the tubes; the same with respect to the others.

To Perform the Experiment.—Bring the bottle forward, and a waiter with three small wine-glasses, · which you fill with the three different liquids, and present the same to the gentlemen. At the same time, ask if the wine is not excellent? One will say, "Very good;" the other, "'Tis nothing but vinegar;" and the third will answer, "'Tis *water!*" You will then feign surprise, and tell them they must be in jest. You now say that you will throw away the contents, and fill the glasses again. This you do, and present wine to the one who had vinegar before, water to the one who had wine, and vinegar to the other, who had water. They will begin to contradict one another. Tell the gentlemen, "Settle the dispute among your-selves. I have tried my best to satisfy you, and am well convinced that the fault must be in your sense of taste: it cannot be my fault. If matters are not all right, I suspect that the wine-sellers have turned jugglers, and played us an odd trick; but I will soon find out, by taking a glass of wine myself,—which he drinks to the health of his audience.

The Inexhaustible Bottle.

THIS well-known trick has many puzzling points for those who witnesss McAllister, Wyman, or Anderson pour over one hundred glasses of liquor from a small bottle; and, what adds to the astonishment of the audience, is to see ten or twenty kinds flow from the

same bottle. The trick is thus explained : The glasses
are so small that a quart bottle will fill seventy-five or
a hundred; the glasses are arranged on a tray in a
• particular manner by the wizard, before the performance begins. The bottle is filled with the following
mixture : spirits-of-wine, water, and sugar; in the
bottom of each glass is a drop or two of Paul de
Veves' Flavoring Extract, as Noyeau, Vanilla, Lemon,
Punch, Essence of Brandy, Port, Sherry, &c. You
are thus enabled to convert a tolerable resemblance of
any fluid that is likely to be called for, and you can
thus supply more than one hundred persons a half sip
of their favorite beverage from the inexhaustible
bottle.

The Egyptian Fluids; or, Impossibilities Accomplished.

AS PERFORMED BY ROBT. HOUDON, OF PARIS.

PROFESSOR HOUDON, a native of France, stands
first among European magicians, and in Paris and
London is exceedingly popular. No professor of the
"black art" has ever equalled him, either in the execution of his tricks, or the accumulation of money;
he being, without doubt, the richest magician in the
world! So great was his popularity, that Louis
Napoleon selected him for a foreign diplomatic mission, and his success was as unexpected as it was
remarkable. By the assistance of his art, he gained
the friendship of the foreign courts, and became at
once flattered and beloved, and consequently accom-

plished the object of his mission, and, on his return, received a very handsome reward for his services.

Mix wine and water together, then separate them by means of a red and white tape. To perform this trick, you must have three covers (tin) made, of an obeliatic form, terminating at about one inch and a half on top; upon the top of two of these covers is soldered a piece of thick brass, copper, or lead, say about a quarter of an inch in thickness; in the centre make a hole about the same in diameter, about two inches from the top, and on the inside will be a partition or floor, through the centre of which make a small hole (this partition must be water-tight). Previous to performing the trick, fill the two covers (the tops of them), one with water, the other with wine; then cork them well, which excludes the air, and consequently keeps the liquid from coming out at the small hole made in the centre of the partition; then take two sound tumblers, and put about as much water in one as there is water in one of the covers; place the cover over that, the tumbler that has the water; then put about the same quantity of wine in the other tumbler as there is in the other cover, and place that cover over it; now have tumbler with a hole through the bottom (made with a drill); have this hole closed with a long peg from the under side; then through your trick-table have a small auger-hole made to admit the peg; this tumbler must also be covered with a similar cover in external appearance. You then take the covers off the tumblers containing water and wine, and, in presence of the audience, mix the two liquids; then pour both into the tumbler that has the hole through the bottom; place the tumblers back, and cover them over; now lift the tumbler up containing the mixture, that the audience may see it (keeping your hand in front of the peg); place it back with peg through the hole, cover it over; then take a red and white tape string that has previously been fastened to a small stick, and place it in the top of the cover that is over the false tumbler; then take the end of the red tape, which has a small wire to it, and, after removing the cork from the cover over the wine, drop the end of the wire into the hole. The air is then let into the wine, which lets it run down into the tumblers underneath. Do likewise with the white tape; then reach your hand under the table and draw the peg out of the tumbler and let the mixture run down into a tumbler or cup secreted there for that purpose; now remove the covers and show the audience that the tumbler you poured the mixture into is empty, and the one you poured it out of contains it again, which will greatly astonish them.

Wyman's Great Disappearance Trick!
AS PERFORMED BY HIM IN ALL THE PRINCIPAL CITIES OF THE UNION.

JOHN WYMAN, JR., the great American Wizard and celebrated Ventriloquist, is, without doubt, more favorably known to the American people than any magician and ventriloquist living, and has been a long time before the public. His performances are so well known and popular, that they require no encomiums from us, and, notwithstanding their frequent repetitions, the same unbounded success is sure to follow each representation. Mr. Wyman had many popular rivals to contend with, but has lived to see the day of his complete triumph, being at this day the greatest magician in America, and probably the most wonderful ventriloquist in the world! In personal appearance Mr. Wyman has the advantage of many of his rivals, having a fine form, pleasing, frank and manly countenance, and a general address almost faultless. No man in the same profession has held higher positions in social life, nor has more warm personal friends. He has played successful engagements in all of the principal places of amusement in the United States, and commanded the highest prices paid the best native artists. Mr. Wyman's performance is unexceptionable in character, and never loses the dignity always found associated with first-class entertainments. His manner is easy, off-hand, and graceful. Quick at repartee, and never at a loss for a word while addressing his audiences. His social converse with his audience has been one principal feature in his exhibitions, making every person present a participator in the amusements of the evening; at home with every one, not haughty or egotistical, and consequently has hosts of friends wherever he performs. He has been offered brilliant engagements in Europe and California; but his great success in this country is probably his chief reason for not accepting the same. To sum up in a few words, Professor Wyman is probably the most successful American magician in the country, having amassed sufficient wealth to place him in an independent position for life.

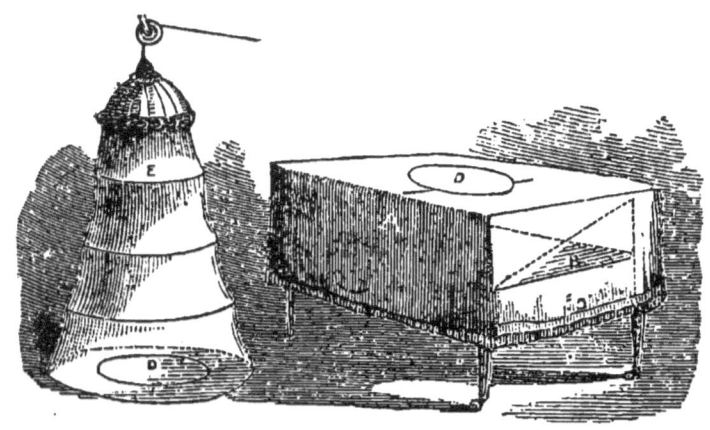

Provide a table with four legs upon castors, marked A, in length 4 feet 6 inches, 3 feet high, 2 feet 4 inches wide—the depth of rim round the table 5 inches, and 2 inches within the edge, as common to most tables. In the top of the table is a round hole 21 inches across, over which is a cover that fits and makes the top appear sound. The cover is connected with the top by two pins, opposite each other, so that pressing the part D, the largest part will be raised. Under the top of the table is a false bottom marked B, attached to the top by a strong cloth, which folds in the middle like a pair of bellows, (represented by the dotted lines), so as to allow the bottom to sink down 18 inches, and guided by grooves in the inner part of the legs of the table. This will leave sufficient room between the top and false bottom to conceal a person. There must be a curtain (marked C) round the table from the top, 20 inches deep, to prevent the false bottom from being seen. When down it is kept up in its place by a couple of buttons on the frame of the table.

The cover is made of black muslin; the bottom is

of wood. The cover is to be 6 feet high, with hoops about 15 inches apart, which will prevent the sack from closing when the sack is extended (see E). The bottom of the cover has a hole the same size as the table, so that when you press on the small part of the cover D, you can raise both covers at the same time.

To Perform this Experiment.—Bring the table forward, and raise the curtain, to convince the company that it is a table of ordinary description. You next show the sack, and strike the bottom to show it is solid wood. Put the sack on the table, exactly over the concealed hole; then let the person who is to disappear step upon the wood bottom of the sack. Then raise the sack over the head, and tie it fast with one end of a rope, one end of which passes through a pulley in the ceiling; then haul the rope tight. In the meantime, the person in the sack treads upon the part of cover marked D, which raises both at once, and allows the person a free passage into the vacant part of the table. The covers will of their own weight fall in their proper place. To move the table from under the sack, say a few magical words, and fire a pistol. Then let the sack fall flat upon the floor.

Herr Alexandre's Mode of Performing the Egg-Bag Trick.

HERR ALEXANDRE is a German by birth, and a rare specimen of the gentleman and scholar, both on and off the stage. He was always dignified in his performance, never descending to the low vulgarity and common-place wit of the buffoon. He at all times was polite, affable, easy, and graceful in manner, and an ornament to his profession. There are many itinerant magicians who have assumed the name of this distinguished gentleman; but the original Herr Alexandre has not been in this country for the past eight or nine years. In personal appearance he was commanding, and added to a large, muscular frame, a stately and erect appearance. His company was courted by the learned of both sexes, and in the private circle he was very witty, and had pleasing conversational powers.

Take a bag and exhibit it to the audience, turn the bag inside-out, then back again, after which take several eggs out of it. To perform this trick, you have a bag about half a yard wide, and about five-eighths deep, made of black cambric; then take strips of the same cloth about three inches wide and sew them on each side of the strip lengthwise of the bag,—these are called cells, it is in these that the eggs are placed; let the end of the cells be closed at the mouth of the large bag, so that the mouth of the cells will be the reverse of that of the large bag,—these are filled with eggs made of wood, with the exception of one or two natural eggs, which they take out first and break, to convince the audience that they are all genuine; when they turn the bag they keep these cells next to them, and as the large bag is turned upside-down, the eggs are in the bottom of the cells at the mouth of the large bag; the performer will then catch the bag just above the eggs, and give it a few raps across the other hand, to convince the audience that there is nothing in it, after which he turns the bag again and takes out several eggs, which to the audience is a great mystery.

Mons. Adrian's Wonderful Feat.
THE ENCHANTED COIN.

MONS. ADRIAN, a Frenchman by birth, was a very skillful magician, and remarkable for his agility and surprising dexterity, though he had reached the advanced age of seventy-seven when I last saw him perform. He was a very popular man in his time, and was very successful in his tour through this country. There are many "Mons. Adrians" at the present day, imitating, but not performing like the original. It is, perhaps, needless to add that those now passing under the name are base *imitators*, and very readily recognized as such when seen by any person at all familiar with Adrian's peculiar style.

Put fifteen pieces of money into a hat, take out five and mysteriously pass them back into the hat, and it covered. To do this trick, you must have in your left hand a plate, and under the plate and in your left hand have previously placed five pieces of coin such as you will have placed in the hat. After you have counted the fifteen pieces into the hat, you then ask the person whom you have selected from the audience to assist you in performing the tricks, to count the money out of the hat into the plate, to see that there is no mistake, after which you turn the money out of the hat into the plate, to see that there is no mistake, after which you turn the money out of the plate into the hat, and at the same time letting fall the five pieces you have secreted in your hand under the plate. You then ask him to draw out five pieces, which will still leave fifteen. You take the five that are drawn out and place them in a drawer (see umbrella factory); then you go through the magic words, *Presto! Pascillo! Pass!* You then open the drawer, (after placing your finger on the spring to hold the inside drawer in which the five pieces were placed,) and show the audience that the five pieces are gone. You then tell him to get the hat and see how many pieces are in it. He gets the hat, and, to the surprise of all, he counts the original number, fifteen.

Astonishing Hindoo Miracle,

PERFORMED BY WILLIAM MARSHALL, THE ORIGINAL FAKIR OF AVA.

WILLIAM MARSHALL, or Marchael, as originally written, was born in Persia. His father, a Scotch officer, married a Persian lady.

Marshall was a very shrewd, far-seeing, ingenious man, and many of our leading theatrical managers will remember his cunning devices to secure to himself the patronage of the public. He once palmed himself on to Mr. Jones, of Vauxhall Garden, New York, as Rahab Ben Marchael, the Arab Magician, and secured a good engagement. Assuming the habits and manners of the Arabs, he was not easily detected. Under this title he created quite an excitement in this country. At another time, he appeared in Baltimore, announced as "a native wealthy citizen, who would transport his audience to the Temple of Ishbaham, in Persia," and all for "the benefit of the poor of the city." The consequence was, the Law Building Hall was nightly crowded, until the disguise was exposed, when he fled to other cities. He was an interesting performer and a good lecturer. There are many counterfeit Fakirs, but none who equal the original. The Fakir died in Louisville, Kentucky, in 1846.

Take a child and place it on a table, then turn a basket over it. The child cries. The performer grows indignant, and pierces a sword through the basket. The child shrieks, and apparently struggles in death. The sword is withdrawn, and blood drips from it. The basket is removed, but no child to be seen. To do this trick, you have to use the trick-table, and also have a confederate. The table is made with a trap-door, fastened on the underside of the table. The child is trained up to the trick, and consequently knows when to cry, and when to not. The child is placed upon the table on the trap-door, at which time it commences to cry. A basket is then placed over it, on the inside of which and next to the performer is fastened a piece of common sponge saturated with blood or its representative. While the performer is making preparation to complete the trick, his confederate opens the trap-door of the table, and lets the child down, but leaves the door open. The child still continues to cry. The performer apparently becomes indignant, and takes a sword and pierces it through the basket, and at the same time through the sponge saturated with blood, at which time the child shrieks.

B

Then the confederate closes the door, which gives the sound of the child a dying appearance. After the sword is withdrawn, the blood that was in the sponge is that which drips from it. This trick produces more terrific sensation than almost any other trick that is performed.

Little Bobby and the Bag.

AS PERFORMED BY SIGNOR BLITZ.

SIGNOR BLITZ came to the United States about twenty-five years since, with an excellent European reputation as a magician, and has won many laurels in addition, while performing in this country. He is now the oldest magician in the United States, and doubtless, equal to the best. He is very eccentric in his habits, but has a kind disposition, frequently aiding the unfortunate and distressed. He has accumulated a large property, owning valuable real estate in Brooklyn and Philadelphia. Mr. Blitz has been one of the most successful performers, pecuniarily speaking, in the country, having, by great perseverance and severe mental application, amassed a handsome fortune. As a performer, he is very pleasing, especially to ladies and children, selecting such experiments as serve to win the child's attention, and likewise enlist the interest of children of a larger growth. He is considered an excellent ventriloquist, and his plate-dancing has never been equalled in America. He has likewise, through patient toil and by dint of the most extraordinary industry, succeeded in learning canary birds to perform the most wonderful feats, and a great portion of his success is, doubtless, to be attributed to these learned canary birds.

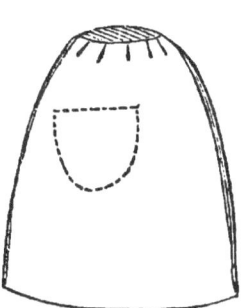

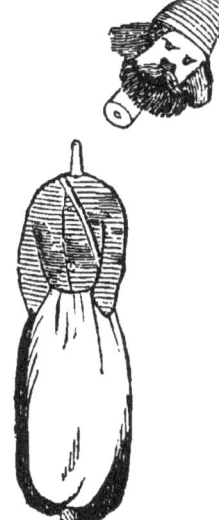

This famous and historical feat (it has been practised in all ages, and in every country under the sun), and perhaps more familiarly known as the "Doll Trick," is thus performed : You must be provided with the figure of a man made of wood, about the size of a small Dutch doll, the head of which takes off and on by means of a peg in the neck, which fits into an aperture in the body. You must also have a cloth cap within for the purpose of concealing the head; but this must be very neatly

constructed, in order that it may not be readily perceived.   Now show your little man to the assembled company, saying, "Gentlemen, I call this my *bonus genius*." Then show the cap, saying, "This, gentlemen, is his coat." Add, "Now look as steadily at him as ever you can, yet, nevertheless, I will deceive you." Then hold the cap above your face, and take the little man in your right hand, and put his head through the hole of the cap, as represented in the engraving. Proceed to describe the doll's virtues as eloquently as you like, saying, "Now, he's a great traveller. He is ready to go any message I like to send him on—to France, to Spain, to Constantinople, to the Crimea, or to the North or South Pole, wherever and whichever you like; but he must have some money to pay his expenses." Then pull out your right hand from under the cap, and with it the body of the doll privately; put your right hand into your pocket (as if you were feeling for money), and leave the body there. Then take your hand out of your pocket, and say, "There is a shilling for you; and now be off on your travels, sir." Then turn the head and say, "But he **must** look about him before he goes. Then say, (setting your forefinger upon his head,) "Just as I thrust my finger down he shall vanish;" and immediately, with the assistance of your left hand, that is under the cap, convey his head into the little bag that is within the cap; then turn the cap about, and, knocking it on the palm of your hand, say, "See, he is gone!" Take your cap and hold it up again, drawing the head out of the little bag, and say, "Hei genius mei velocissimus, ubi," and give a whistle; at the same time thrust the head up through the hole in the cap, and hold the head by the peg, and turn it about. You can thus cause the doll to appear and disappear as many times as you like, to the great amazement and bewilderment of the company.

The Mysterious Desk.

PERFORMED BY PROFESSOR HARRINGTON.

JONATHAN HARRINGTON, the New England Magician and Ventriloquist, was born in Boston, Mass., and has been many years before the public of New England. He commenced his career at a very early age, and his course has been onward and upward until at the present day he stands without a rival in New England. Mr. Harrington was at one time the proprietor of the New England Museum, located in Boston. He has had a very successful career, and in the summer months rusticates at his fine country-seat in Chelsea, Mass. As a performer he is very excellent, and gives general satisfaction to a promiscuous audience.

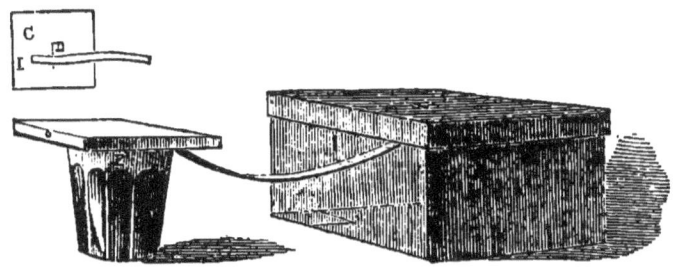

Have a box made with a lock, five inches long, three inches wide, and three inches deep. Have a hole at the bottom, (as at A,) one inch square with a piece of wood that will fit the vacancy, and resemble the box. It must be hung on small hinges, (as marked B,) so that you can raise the block with your finger. It will fall of itself in its place. Have a block three inches square (marked C), with a hole (D) one inch long, nearly as deep and a little wider than a dime.

Have, also, a riband one yard long, and fastened to the board (C) at E; then all is ready for the experiment. Request one of the company to mark a dime, so that it may be identified, and let it be thrown into the box; put the loose end of the riband into the box, and request him to lock the same and keep the key; then raise, secretly, the swinging-board (B), and shake the box, so that the spectators are assured that the coin is inside; let the coin, at the same time, drop through the hole into your own hand, where you conceal it. Then place the box on the table, and take the piece of wood (C) which has the other end of the riband fastened to it. Lay the board over a tumbler, with the marked side down (F), or that side down which has the end of the riband fastened at E and the hole (D); at the same time, secretly put the coin with the bend of the riband into the hole (D). Place the tumbler from the box, nearly at the distance the riband will now admit, and request two of the company to come forward. Let one of them put his hand on the board (C), which now covers the tumbler, while the other person holds his hand on the box; then take the magic rod in your hand, and pass it back and forward under the riband, pronouncing some magic words; give a sudden jerk upon the riband, which will pull the bend with the coin out of the hole (D); the coin will then fall in the tumbler. Give it back to the owner, who will acknowledge that it is the same that he dropped into the box. Ask for the key, open the box, and you'll convince the assembly that nothing is there.

Professor Jacobs' Lesson on Cooking.

JACOBS, now in California, is a Jew by birth, and has a great reputation in England, Ireland, and Scotland. He is reputed to be in possession of a magnificent apparatus, with which he does many very wonderful things.

Take a saucepan, like A, with a long handle, ten inches across the top and six inches deep; have a cover, as B, with a rim round it, C, two inches deep, with a piece of tin, D, which will fit the inside of rim, C. Now fill the secret part, between the real cover, B, and the tin, D, with sugar-plums or kisses. Always keep the cover on your table. Cut up potatoes and apples in your saucepan, A, and hand it round to the company for inspection. Return to the table, put on your cover, B, well over a candle, so that the tin, D, will fall down and expose the candy. Take off the cover, and present the confectionery to the audience on plates, keeping the saucepan on the table to prevent the trick from being discovered.

Herr Dobler's Coffee and Tea Exchange.

HERR DOBLER, a very popular German magician, has never visited the United States. He stands high in his profession, and is, no doubt, a very excellent conjurer.

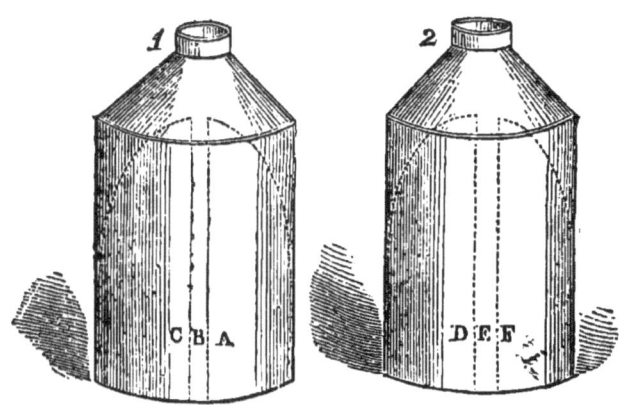

Have two canisters made twelve inches high, including the top, four and a half inches in diameter; the straight sides being ten inches in height, divided across the inside in three separate apartments, as A, B, C—the middle division being half an inch wide one way, and the width of the canister the other. A and C are of equal dimensions. The divisions that form the apartment, B, is nine inches high from the bottom. The parts A and C have a division sloping down, as represented in the cuts. Having described the construction of the apparatus, now put in A coffee, and tea in C, the raw material on the liquid, the same in D and F. By turning can No. 1 to the right slowly, you pour out the coffee on a plate,—the tea contained in the opposite apartment will not run out. Then turn can No. 2 to the left, and the tea will appear on the plate. Then replace the tea and coffee, by means of a funnel, in their respective places. Say some unmeaning words, and tip canister No. 1 to the left and

No. 2 to the right, and, to the amazement of the audience, the change will appear to have taken place. By the same canisters you may produce hot coffee, milk, &c.

Joe Pentland's Favorite Trick.

TO PUT A RING THROUGH ONE'S CHEEK.

JOE PENTLAND, the famous circus clown, now in Europe and creating a sensation, was once a magician, travelling with P. T. Barnum, but subsequently relinquished the practice of magic for the circus-ring, where he became eminent and won his present celebrity.

This is on the same principle as the preceding. You must have two rings exactly alike, one of which has a notch, which admits your cheek. When you have exhibited the perfect ring, you change it for the other, and privately slip the notch over one side of your mouth; in the meantime you slip the whole ring on your stick, hiding it with your hand; then desire some one to hold the end of the stick, whip the ring out of your cheek, and smite with it instantly upon the stick, concealing it, and whirling the other ring, which you hold your hand over, round about the stick

Professor Davidson's Bottle Imp.

AS MADE BY HIM AT BARNUM'S AMERICAN MUSEUM, NEW YORK.

GET three little hollow figures of glass, an inch and a half high, representing Imps, or Harlequin, Columbine, and Pantaloon, which may be obtained of the glass-blowers, with a small hole in each of their legs. Immerge them into water contained in a glass bottle, which should be about fifteen inches high, and covered with a bladder tied fast over the top. A small quantity of air must be left between the bladder and the surface of the water. When you think fit to command the figures to go down, press your hand hard upon the top, and they will immediately sink.

Xavier Chaubert's Trick.

HOW TO EAT FIRE.

MONS. CHAUBERT, a Frenchman, was the original "Fire King" in this country, being the first man who introduced experiments with fire, heat, and poisons. He would enter a heated oven of 500 degrees Fahrenheit, drink prussic acid, eat phosphorous, claiming to have an antidote for any poison, however deadly. Drs. Houton and Devine also discovered the secret of eating fire, &c., and successfully performed the same extraor-

dinary feats. The secret of their performances we
expose below :—

Anoint your tongue with liquid storax, and you
may put a pair of red hot tongs into your mouth, and
without hurting yourself, and lick them till they are
cold. You may also take coals out of the fire, and
eat them as you would bread. Dip them into brim-
stone-powder, and the fire will seem more strange, but
the sulphur puts out the coal; and if you shut your
mouth close, you put out the sulphur, and so chew the
coals and swallow them, which you may do without
offending the body. If you put a piece of lighted
charcoal into your mouth, you may suffer a pair of
bellows to be blown into your mouth continually, and
receive no hurt; but your mouth must be quickly
cleaned, otherwise it will cause a salivation. This is a
very dangerous trick to be done, and those who practice it ought to use all means they can to prevent
danger. I never saw one of these fire-eaters that had
a good complexion.

Professor Whitney's Great Trick of Passing a Handkerchief into a Bottle of Wine.

PROFESSOR WHITNEY, otherwise known as the
" Wierd Man," is very popular in the South and West,
and enjoys a good reputation generally. He is a good
necromancer,—skillful and clever. His head-quarters
are at Detroit, Michigan, though he occasionally gets
off to Toledo, Cleveland, and even as far north as
Pittsburg. We never saw him perform farther north,

and believe his old stamping-ground to be South-west and West.

Place two bottles of wine on the small table; give previously to the secret agent an empty bottle similar to the others, a tin tube closed at one end, three inches long, that will fit into the neck, and a glass of wine. The performer borrows a handkerchief, and makes it disappear on the table as in the former experiment. The secreted person puts the handkerchief through the neck into the empty bottle; puts the tube which he fills with wine, and places it in the neck close to the mouth of the bottle, into which he puts a cork. The performer states that he will now produce the handkerchief from one of those bottles standing on the table, with which he has had no connection. He takes one in each hand, and, in passing round the table, one of them is exchanged for the concealed one. He steps before the audience and states that he has two bottles of wine, and proposes to drink the company's health. He draws the cork, and pours out into a glass, which he tastes, but remarks that it is not good,—I will try the other, which he does, and pronounces it to be excellent. He says, "Ladies and gentlemen, in which of those two bottles shall I find the handkerchief?" They answer variously, which gives the performer the chance to select the right one. This he breaks and produces the handkerchief, and throws the broken glass with the tube aside, so that it shall not be discovered. He now breaks the other bottle, and the company see it contained nothing but wine. He now leaves it to the audience to find out the deception the best way they can.

Cut a Handkerchief in Pieces, and make it Whole again.

PERFORMED BY MONS. PHILLIPPI.

MONS. PHILLIPPI, a French magician, unable to speak the English language, came to this country about fifteen years ago. He performed in several of our large cities; but, owing to his lack of knowledge of our language, was compelled to return to France, unsuccessful. Phillippi was a very clever magician, an ingenious mechanic and an excellent chemist. He was the inventor of the "Orange Tree," and first introduced this beautiful illusion to the public.

This feat, strange as it appears, is very simple. The performer must have a confederate, who has two handkerchiefs of the same quality, and with the same mark, one of which he throws upon the stage to perform the feat with. The performer takes care to put this handkerchief uppermost in making the bundle, though he affects to mix them together promiscuously. The person whom he desires to draw one of the handkerchiefs naturally takes that which comes first to his hand. He desires him to shake them again to embellish the operation, but, in so doing, takes care to bring the right handkerchief uppermost, and carefully fixes upon some simpleton to draw; and if he finds that he is not likely to take the first that comes to his hand, he prevents him from drawing by fixing upon another, under pretence of his having a more sagacious look. When the handkerchief is torn and carefully folded up, it is put under a glass upon a table near a partition. On that part of the table on which it is deposited is a little trap, which opens and lets it fall into a drawer. The confederate, concealed behind the curtain, passes his hand within the table, opens the trap, and substitutes the second handkerchief instead of the first; then shuts the trap, which fits so exactly the hole it closes, as to deceive the eyes of the most incredulous. If the performer be not possessed of such a table, (which is absolutely necessary for other feats as well as this,) he must have the second handkerchief in his pocket, and by sleight-of-hand change it for the pieces, which must be instantaneously concealed.

To Pass a Block of Wood from One Hat into Another.

PERFORMED BY J. H. McCANN.

Joseph H. McCann, the Western Magician, is a native of Baltimore. He commenced his profession at a very early age, and has been before the public for upwards of twenty years. He is a man of great versatility of talent, being at once a magician, equilibrist, musician, singer, and mimic. He can take-off actors, imitate Dr. Valentine, perform various gymnastics, sing a good song, play on any instrument, tell a good story, play a good sleight-of-hand trick, and, to conclude, is a good, whole-souled, social fellow. He confines himself to Kentucky, Ohio, Indiana, and Missouri.

Procure a pasteboard box four inches square, open at the top, marked A ; have a second one made of tin, B, that will exactly fit in A, with the outside painted black, and ornamented to suit taste in white. Then have a solid block of wood, C, which will exactly fit figure, B, so that it may be slipped in or out at pleasure.   The block, C, must be painted the same as B.

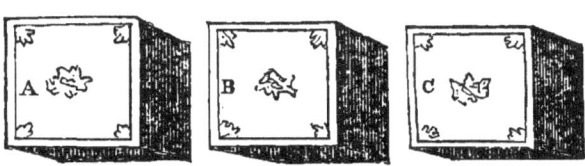

To Perform the Experiment.—Have the block C covered with B; show the company that it is a solid block of wood, A being the cover.   Borrow two hats, —take one of them in your hand, and hold the inside a little toward you; next take the box B between your finger, and press it so that the block C will be with it.   Now put the block in the hat, pretending to try if the hat is large enough to hold it.   In doing so, let your fingers loose, and the solid block C will fall from the box B into the hat.   Then raise B, and it will appear the same as before.   Be careful not to expose the open part.   Now set the hat containing the block C upon the table; place a plate on the hat, and the second hat crown-up upon the plate.   Take B in your hand, and place on the crown of the hat.   Then cover B with the pasteboard cover A.   Say a few magical words.   Then lift the pasteboard box from the hat, pressing the fingers tightly, so as to retain B inside of A.   The solid block C will apparently have disappeared, and, to the astonishment of all, will be found in the bottom hat, which you can show with the block to the company for examination.

The Penetrative Shilling.

PERFORMED BY OTIS EVERETT.

EVERETT, the great Southern Magician, is a very popular man in North and South Carolina, Georgia, Alabama, and Florida; in which States he usually exhibits. He is a very skillful necromancer, and has accumulated considerable wealth by his performances. He is a very shrewd business man, and knows how to preserve what he earns. He is now the owner of several successful canvas-shows travelling through the Southern country.

Provide a round tin box, of the size of a large snuff-box, and likewise eight other boxes, which will easily fit into each other, and let the least of them be of a size to hold a shilling. Each of these boxes should shut with a hinge, and to the least of them there must be a small lock, fastened with a spring, but which cannot be opened without a key, and observe that all these boxes must shut so freely that they may all be closed at once. Place these boxes in each other, with their tops open, in your pocket; then ask a person for a shilling, and desire him to mark it, that it may not be changed; take this piece in one hand, and in the other have another of the same appearance, and, in putting your hand in your pocket, you slip the piece that is marked into the least box, and, shutting them all at once, you take them out; then, showing the piece you have in your hand, and which the company suppose to be the same that was marked, you pretend to make it pass through the box, but dexterously convey it away. You then present the box, for the spectators do not know yet that there are more than one, to any person in the company, who, when he opens it, finds another and another, till he comes to the last, but that he cannot open without the key, which you then give him; and, retiring to a distant part of the room, you tell him to take out the shilling himself, and see if it be the one marked.   This trick may be made more surprising by putting the key into the snuff-box of one of the company; which you may do by asking for a pinch of snuff; the key, being very small, will lie concealed among the snuff.   When the person who opens the boxes asks for the key, tell him that one of his friends has it in his snuff-box.

Scrap, or Blowing Book.
PERFORMED BY POTTER.

POTTER, or "Old Black Potter," as he was called, has been dead nearly twenty years, though his name is to this day as familiar as a household word with some of the old New England residents.   The New Englanders believe there was never a greater juggler existed than Potter, and we venture to assert that he had no superior in his line.   He was a very comical performer, and done many of his tricks very handsomely. Though a *black* man, he was master of the "Black Art" and few white performers of his day could equal him in the execution of his surprising feats.   Potter died about twenty years ago, at his handsome residence, in Massachusetts.

Take a book seven inches long, and about five inches
c

broad, and let there be forty-nine leaves, that is seven times seven contained therein, so as you may cut upon the edges of each leaf six notches, each notch in depth of a quarter of an inch, with a gouge made for that purpose, and let them be one inch distant ; paint every thirteenth or fourteenth page, which is the end of every sixth leaf and beginning of every seventh, with like colours or pictures ; cut off with a pair of scissors every notch of the first leaf, leaving one inch of paper, which will remain half a quarter of an inch above that leaf ; leave another like inch in the second part of the second leaf, clipping away an inch of paper in the highest place above it, and all notches below the same, and orderly to the third and fourth, and so there shall rest upon each leaf only one nick of paper above the rest, one high uncut, an inch of paper must answer to the first directly, so as when you have cut the first seven leaves in such a manner as described, you are to begin the self same order at the eighth leaf, descending the same manner to the cutting other seven leaves to twenty-one, until you have passed through every leaf all the thickness of your book.

Dr. James Wyman's Laughing-Gas.

DR. WYMAN of New England, was an experienced Chemist, Alchemist and Natural Philosopher. He introduced the laughing-gas to the public in all the principal cities of the United States, and met with great success. Although bearing the same name as " Wyman the Wizard," he is not related to that gentleman.

The above fanciful appellation has been given to nitrous oxide, from the agreeable sensations excited by inhaling it.   In its pure state it destroys animal life, but loses this noxious quality when inhaled, because it becomes blended with the atmospheric air which it meets in the lungs.   This gas is made by putting three or four drachms of nitrate of ammonia, in crystals, into a small glass retort, which being held over a spirit lamp, the crystals will melt, and the gas be dissolved. Having thus produced the gas, it is to be passed into a large bladder having a stop-cock ; and when you are desirous of exhibiting its effect, you cause the person who wishes to experience them to first exhale the atmospheric air from the lungs, and then quickly placing the cock in his mouth, you turn it, and bid him inhale the gas.   Immediately, a sense of extraordinary cheerfulness, fanciful flights of imagination, an uncontrollable propensity to laughter, and a consciousness of being capable of great muscular exertion, supervene.   It does not operate exactly in the same manner on all persons, but in most cases the sensations are agreeable, and have this important difference from those produced by wine or spirituous liquors—that they are not succeeded by any depression of mind.

Wonderful Decapitation Feat!
AS PERFORMED BY THE CHINESE JUGGLERS.

The Chinese Jugglers first appeared in California direct from China where they created an immense excitement by the performance of the decapitation and

impalement feats.   Their feats of legerdemain however,
were inferior to those performed by many of the English and American Necromancers.   Dr. Ghion, then
in California, aware of their immense popularity, secured them for a tour through the States, commencing
at New Orleans, and visited every city in succession
from New Orleans to the confines of Maine, creating a
perfect *furore* of excitement.   This company soon dis-
banded, their performances not admitting of repeti-
tion, and the different members of the once popular
band are now scattered around in different portions of
our country—several of them now to be seen in New
York, peddling cigars for a livelihood !

    This is a curious performance if it be handled by a
skilful hand.   To show this feat of execution, you must
cause a board, a cloth, and a platter to be purposely
made, and in each of them to be made holes fit for a
person's neck ; the board must be made of two planks,
the longer and broader the better ; there must be left
within half a yard of the end of each plank half a hole,
so as both the planks being thrust together, there may
remain two holes, like holes in a pair of stocks, there
must be made likewise a hole in the cloth ; a platter
also must be set directly over or upon one of them,
having a hole in the middle thereof, of the like quantity, and also a piece cut off the same, as big as his
neck, through which his head may be conveyed into the
middle of the platter, and then sitting or kneeling under
the board, let the head only remain upon the board-
in the frame.   Then to make the sight more striking,
put a little brimstone into a chafing-dish of coals, sit-

ting it before the head of the boy, who must gasp two or three times, so as the smoke may enter his nostrils and mouth, which is not unwholesome, and the head presently will appear stark dead, if the boy act his countenance accordingly, and if a little blood be sprinkled on his face the sight will be stranger. This is commonly practised with a boy instructed for that purpose, who being familiar and conversant with company, may be known as well by his face as by his apparel. In the other end of the table, where the like hole is made, another boy of the bigness of the known boy must be placed, having on his usual apparel : he must lean or lie upon the board, and must put his head under it through the side hole, so as the body shall seem to lie on the end of the board, and his head lie in a platter on the other end. There are other things which might be performed in this action, the more to astonish the beholders, which, because they require long descriptions, are here omitted ; as to put about his neck a little dough kneaded with bullock's blood, which being cold, will appear like dead flesh, and being pricked with a sharp round hollow quill, will bleed and seem very strange ; and many rules are to be observed herein, as to have the table-cloth so long and so wide as it may almost reach the ground.

The Orange Tree Illusion.
AS EXHIBITED BY MONS. ADONIS.

Mons. Adonis, the French Wizard, first appeared in New Orleans, where he became very popular, especially with the French population : he afterwards started on a tour through the Northern States, but being unable to speak English sufficiently well to make his audience understand resorted to his native dialect, which was explained to the audience generally by an interpeter, who spoke English but little better than the Monsieur. The result was, he met with but poor success, and after repeated failures and heavy losses, packed up his apparatus and sailed back to France. Adonis was an excellent magician, a perfect master of his art, and had he learned the English language before he sailed for America, would have made one of the most successful tours ever made by a foreigner in this country. As it is, he has returned to his native land broken down in fortune, dispirited, and forced to manual labor, for the support of his family.

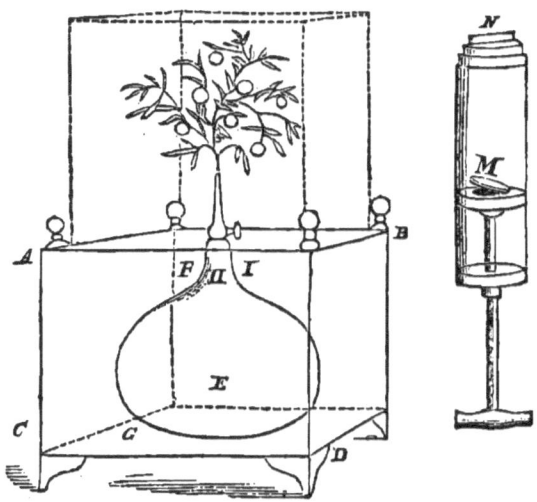

Make a box, A, B, C, of about six inches every way, in the middle of the top A, B, let there be a hole, through which is to pass the neck of the vessel E, that is a kind of hollow copper sphere, of four inches in diameter, and covered at its top and bottom, F and G, with two pieces of the same metal.   To the part next to F, there is to be a tube H., about half an inch in diameter, through which is an aperture of a quarter of an inch ; this tube must also be pierced horizontally, by an opening of one-third of an inch at I, to admit a lock, the key of which must extend to the outside of the case.   It should also have a small aperture of about one-tenth of an inch to let out the air that is to be compressed in the vessel E, as we shall now explain.

To force the air into the hollow vessel there must be adjusted to one of its sides the copper syringe, N M, which has a little valve at M, and at the extremity N, so that by alternately thrusting in and drawing out the piston, the air may be strongly condensed in the vessel E.

To the extremity of the tube H, there is fixed the little tree O, which is composed of four or five branches of copper that proceed from the stem O, these branches are hollow that the air that enters the bottom may extend to the top.   To these branches are adjusted twigs, made of brass wire, and the whole decorated with orange leaves made of parchment, and coloured to imitate nature.

The ends of the branches are to dilate, so as to contain small pieces of fine kid, which are to take the figure of an orange when they are extended by the air drove through the branches.   These oranges of kid must be contained within the extremity of the branches to which they are fastened by a silk thread, and there

must be a space left at the ends of the branches to
which is to be fixed the bud and flower of a blowing
orange.   The trunk of the tree must fit the tube H
that none of the air may escape.   The branches and
kid that are to form the oranges must be accurately
painted so as to favor the illusion.   The whole to
be covered by a glass case, to prevent any one touching it.

Previous to performing this trick, with a little stick,
put the kid oranges within the end of each branch ;
also the flowers of the blowing orange, that no part
may appear.   You then fill the vessel by means of the
syringe with air.

Matters being thus arranged introduce the box and
tree covered with the glass shade, and show the company the present state—that it bears neither flowers
nor fruit—tell them it shall instantly produce both.
You then turn the cock, when the flowers and buds
will immediately appear, and will be succeeded by the
fruit.

THE

COMPLETE HISTORY AND EXPOSURE

OF

VENTRILOQUISM.

Containing a full account of the wonderful powers of the human voice ; an epitome of all the most distinguished ventriloquists in the world ; the arts practiced to obtain ventriloquial power ; the different theories of celebrated men, in reference to the faculty of sound in the human voice ; a detailed explanation of the easiest mode of acquiring the faculty of throwing the voice; the mechanical contrivances of ingenious and talented persons ; how to become a practical ventriloquist ; dialogues for public exhibition ; also a variety of experiments, and ideas never before published, concerning the startling and amusing faculties possessed by a ventriloquist. The whole compiled and arranged from Professor Wyman's extensive library of works on the arts and sciences; and from private manuscripts of celebrated ventriloquists; also, Prof. Wyman's mode of performing ventriloquism,

BY E. MASON, JR.

———

PHILADELPHIA :

1860.

"AND THOU SHALT BE BROUGHT DOWN, *and* SHALL SPEAK OUT OF THE GROUND, AND THY SPEECH SHALL BE LOW OUT OF THE DUST, AND THY VOICE SHALL BE, AS OF ONE THAT HATH A FAMILIAR SPIRIT, OUT OF THE GROUND, AND THY SPEECH SHALT WHISPER OUT OF THE DUST."—*Isaiah*, xxix. 4.

The practitioner of this occult art, is well known to have a power of modifying his voice in such a manner, as to imitate the voices of different persons conversing at a considerable distance from each other, and in very different tones. And hence the first impression which this ingenious trick or exhibition produced on the world, was that of the artist's possessing a double or triple Larynx; the additional larynxes being supposed to be seated still deeper in the chest than the lowermost of the two that belong to birds; whence indeed the name of ventriloquism or belly-speaking.

Mr. Gough has attempted in the memoirs of the Manchester Society, to resolve the whole into the phenomena of echoes; the ventriloquist being conceived by him on all occasions to confine himself to a room well disposed for echoes in various parts of it, and merely to produce false voices by directing his natural voice in a straight line towards such echoing parts instead of in a straight line towards the audience; who upon this view of the subject, are supposed to be artfully placed on one or both sides of the ventriloquist. It is sufficient to observe, in opposition to this conjecture, that it does not account for the perfect quiescence of the mouth and cheeks of the performer while employing his feigned voices; and that an adept in the

art, is wholly indifferent to the room in which he prac-
tices, and will allow another person to choose a room
for him.

Mr. Richerand, one of the most popular French physiologists of the day, who has examined the vocal organs
of several ventriloquists, observes, as the results of his
investigation, that although there is little or no motion
in the cheeks during the act of speaking, there is considerable demand and expenditure of air ; the ventriloquist always inhaling deeply before he commences his
deception, passing a part of the air thus inhaled through
his nostrils, and being able to continue his various
voices as long as the inspired air may last, or till he
has inhaled a fresh supply.

This view of the subject induced Mr. Richerand to
relinquish the old hypothesis of a kind of vocal organ
being seated in the stomach, to which we have already
adverted, and which he had formerly embraced ; though
it does not appear that he has very distinctly adopted
any other in its stead ; "At first," says he, "I had
conjectured that a great part of the air expelled by
expiration did not pass out by the mouth and nostrils,
but was swallowed and carried into the stomach ; and
being reflected in some part of the digestive canal,
gives rise to a real echo ; but after having more attentively observed this curious phenomenon, I was soon
convinced that the name of ventriloquism is by no
means applicable ; since the whole of its mechanism
consists in a slow, gradual expiration ; in which the
artist either influences at his will the surrounding
muscles of the chest, or keeps down the epiglottis by

the base of the tongue, the point of which is not pro-
tracted beyond the arch of the teeth."

M. de la Chapelle, without offering any particular
explanation of this curious art, published in 1772, an
ingenious work, in which he attempted to prove that
ventriloquism is of a very ancient date ; and that it
formed the mode by which the responses of many of
oracles of former times were delivered by the priests
and priestesses, to the credulous multitudes around
them.   And although this able writer has not fully
succeeded in establishing his point, it must be allowed
by every one, that no art, while it continued occult,
would better answer the purpose of such sort of imposition ; for an adept in the science is capable of
modulating and inflecting his voice with so nice a
dexterity, as not only to imitate with equal accuracy,
the cries of dogs, cats, infants, and all persons in dis-
tress, together with every modification of articulate
speech, but apparently to throw the mimic sound from
whatever quarter he chooses ; from the ceiling or roof
of a house, the corner of the room, the mouths, the
stomachs, or pockets of any of the company present,
from their hands or feet, from beneath a hat or glass,
or from a wooden doll.   A humorous artist of this
kind is said to have amused himself some years ago, by
frequenting the fish market at Edinburgh, and making
a fish speak, and give its vender the lie in her own
gross preaching, upon her affirming that it was fresh,
and caught in the morning ; the fish quaintly replying
as often as she so asserted that it had been dead for a
week, and that she knew it.

It is certain that hitherto, no satisfactory explanation

has been offered of this singular phenomenon ; and I shall, therefore, take leave to suggest that it is, possibly, of a much simpler character than has usually been apprehended ; that the entire range of its imitative power is confined to the larynx alone, and that the art itself consists in a close attention to the almost infinite variety of tones, articulations, and inflections the larynx is capable of producing in its own region, when long and dexterously practised upon, and a skilful modification of these effects into mimic speech, passed for the most part, and whenever necessary, through the cavity of the nostrils, instead of through the mouth. The parrot in imitating human language, employs the larynx and nothing else ; as does the mocking-bird, the most perfect ventriloquist in nature in imitating cries and imitations of all kinds.

Every bird keeper knows that it is not necessary for birds to open their bills in the act of singing, except for the purpose of uttering the note already formed in the larynx, that would otherwise have to pass through the nostrils, which, in birds, prove a much less convenient passage for the sound than in man ; and of so little use is the tongue towards the formation of sound, that instances are not wanting of birds that have continued their song after they have lost the entire tongue by accident or disease. It is said that the ventriloquist, on many occasions does not use the tongue, which is false ; the tongue is equally necessary to inarticulate and to articulate language. But all musical sounds may be produced without the aid of the tongue, the larynx is the sole organ. All natural cries, even though modulated by music, are from the throat and larynx

or knot of the throat, with little or no operation of
the organs of the mouth.   But of the twenty-four
articulate sounds which the alphabet comprises, there
are but few in which the tongue takes a distinct lead,
as in the *l, d, t,* &c., though it is auxiliary to several
others ; but the guttural or polatine, *g, h, k, q, ;* the
nasal, as *m,* and *n, ;* the labial, as *b, p; f, v,* and most
of the dental, together with all the vowels, are but
little indebted to its assistance.   I see no reason why
the ventriloquist should not use his tongue : it is not
seen by the audience when exercising his art ; certain
it is the ventriloquist when holding a conversation
with supposed personages does not, or ought not to
use the lips or let the muscles of the face be seen to
move, as the deception would not be complete ; the
imagination of the audience could not be kept in play
to fancy the voice from the quarter the ventriloquist
wishes it to appear.

When speaking in a ventriloquial voice I compress
the teeth firm together which contracts the muscles of
the face and keeps them from vibrating with the voice,
this is all the ventriloquist wants, *viz :* When conversing with supposed personages, during their answers to
keep the muscles of the face and lips perfectly still,
and to let the conversation be so arranged that the
letters *b, f, m, p, v,* are seldom if ever used ; but
when they are used, I give my face an impassive
expression ; or one very foreign to the verbal expression
to which I am giving utterance.   Anatomists mention
two instances of persons speaking without a tongue.
In one case the organ, was originally wanting, but its
place was supplied by a small tubercle and the rivala

was perfect.   In the other the tongue was destroyed by disease.*

The tongue is a natural and common organ in the functions of the voice, &c., and is absolutely necessary in all articulate tones.

The term ventriloquist, and other words of similar import were employed, in the infancy of the science, but it is evident that we ought not to admit them now in scientific language : for the art of the ventriloquist does not, (according to the derivation of the word,) consists in speaking in the belly, but when stifled sounds are formed in the larynx, and articulated without moving the muscles of the face, he gives them strength by a powerful action of the abdominal muscles.   Hence he speaks by means of his belly, although the throat is the real source from which the sounds proceed.   This art does not depend on a particular structure or organ-ization of the nerves and muscles of the throat, but may be acquired by many, to a certain extent, while others do not, nor *can ever* possess ; in the same manner as it makes some capable of singing, whilst others are ever incapacitated.   But there is a great degree of obscure action about the parts composing the vocal tube,† which none but the practitioner with

---

* Good's Book of Nature, page 260.

† Well may the deceptions that are practised with the human voice take place when fifteen of different muscles are attached to the cartilages, or to the osyhoides, and acting as agents, antagonists, or directors, are constantly employed in keeping the cartilages steady, in regulating their situation, and moving them as occasion requires,—upward and down-ward, backward and forward and in every intermediate

immense practice and study is able to comprehend and put in force, especially when regulating the distant voice to make it appear nearer, and which voice cannot be produced by the action of the glottis alone. The glottis in the production of acute sounds is contracted but instead of descending in the case of acute tones and in rising in that of the grave, the reverse is the fact. Thus the art of the ventriloquist consists,

First, In modifying his voice according to the different variations, or changes, the supposed person is thought to occupy.

Second, In keeping the imagination of his auditors in play, and attracting their attention with a degree of *finesse* only to be acquired by repeated trials, and intense practise and study.

---

direction, according to the course of the muscular fibres, or in the diagonal between different fibres. These muscles independently of the former, are susceptible of upwards of 1.073,841,800 different combinations; and when they co-operate with the seven pairs of larynx, of 17.592,186,044,415; exclusive of the changes which must arise from the different degrees of force, velocity, &c., with which they may be brought into action. But these muscles are not the whole that co-operate with the larynx, in the production of the voice. The diaphragm the abdominal muscles, the inter-costals, and all that directly or indirectly act on the air or on the parts to which the muscles of the glottis or oshyoides are attached,—in short all the muscles that recover nerves from the respiratory system contribute their share. The numerical estimate would consequently, require to be largely augmented. Such calculations are of course, only approximate, but they show the inconceivable variety of movement of which the vocal apparatus is directly or indirtctly suscep-tible.

D

Third, In keeping the muscles of the face &c., in a state of composure, during the answer of the supposed party.

FROM GOOD'S BOOK OF NATURE.

At the root of the tongue lies a minute semi-lunar shaped bone, which from its resemblance to the Greek letter ѵ, or upsilon, is called the hyoid or u-likebone ; and immediately from this bone arises a long cartila-ginous tube, which extends to the lungs, and conveys the air backward and forward in the process of respira-tion. This tube is denominated the trachæa or wind-pipe ; and the upper part of it, or that immediately connected with the hyoid-bone, the larynx : and it is this upper part or larynx alone that constitutes the seat of the voice.

The tube of the larynx, short as it is, is formed of five distinct cartilages ; the largest and apparently, though not really, lowermost of which, produces that acute projection or knot in the anterior part of the neck, and especially in the neck of the males, of which every one must be sensible. This is not a complete ring, but is open behind : the open space being filled up, in order to make a complete ring, with other two cartilages of a smaller size and power ; and what to-gether form the glottis, as it is called, or aperture out of the mouth into the larynx. The fourth cartilage lies immediately over this aperture, and closes in the act of swallowing, so as to direct the food to the esophagus, another opening immediately behind it, which leads to the stomach. These four cartilages are supported by a fifth, which constitutes their basis ; and is narrow before, and broad behind, and has some resemblance to a seal-ring. The larynx is contracted and dilated in a variety of ways by the antagonist power of different muscles, and the elasticity of its cartilaginous coats; and is covered internally with a very sensbile, vascular, and mucous membrane which is a continuation of the membrane of the mouth. The organ of the voice then is the larynx, its muscles, and appendages: and the voice itself is the sound of the air propelled through and striking against the sides of its glottis; or opening into the mouth. The shrillness or roughness of the voice depends on the internal diameter of the glottis, its elasticity, mobility, and lubricity, and the force with which the air is protruded. Speech is the modification of the voice into distinct articulations, in the locality of the glottis itself, or in that of the mouth, or of the nostrils. Those animals only that possess lungs possess a larynx, and hence none but the first three classes in the Linnæan system, consisting of mammals, birds and amphibials. Even among these however, some gender or species are entirely dumb, as the myrmecophaga or ant-eater, the manis or pomgolin, and the cetaceous tribes, together with the tortoise, lizards, and serpents; while others lose their voice in particular regions; as the dog is said to do in some parts of America; and quails and frogs in various districts of Siberia.

It is from the greater or less degree of perfection with which the larynx is formed in the different classes of animals that possess it, that the voice is rendered more or less perfect; and it is by an introduction of superadded membranes, or muscles, into its general structure, or a variation in the shape, position, or

elasticity of those that are common to it, that quadrupeds and other animals are capable of making those
peculiar sounds, by which their different kinds, are
respectively characterized, and are able to neigh, bray,
bark or roar ; to pur as the cat and tiger kind, to bleat
as the sheep, or to croak as the frog.

The larynx of the bird class is of a very peculiar
form, and admirably adapted to that sweet and varied
music with which we are so often delighted in the
woodlands.   In reality the whole extent of the trachea
or windpipe in birds may be regarded as one vocal
apparatus ; for the larynx is divided into two sections,
or may rather, perhaps, be considered as two distinct
organs ; the more complicated, or that in which the
parts are more numerous and elaborate, being placed
at the bottom of the trachea, when it divides into two
branches, one for each of the lungs : and the simpler,
or that in which the parts are fewer, and consist of
those not included in the former, occupying its usual
situation at the uper end of the trachea, which however,
is without an epiglottis ; the food and other substances
being incapable of entering the aperture of the glottis
from another contrivance.   The lungs, trachea, and
larynx of birds, therefore, may be regarded as forming
a complete natural bagpipe ; in which the lungs con-
stitute the pouch and supply the wind ; the trachea
itself the pipe ; the inferior glottis the head or mouth
piece, which produces the simple sound ; and the superior glottis the finger-holes, which modify the simple
sound into an infinite variety of distinct notes, and at
the same time give them utterance.

Among the bird-tribes there are some possessed of

powers of voice so singular, independently of that of their own natural music, that I cannot consent to pass them over in total silence. The note of the pipra musica, or tuneful manakin, is not only intrinsically sweet, but forms a complete octave ; one note succeeding another in ascending and measured intervals through the whole range of its diapason. This bird is an inhabitant of St. Domingo, of a black tint, with a blue crown and yellow front and hump ; about four inches long, very shy, and dexterous in eluding the vigilance of such as attempt to take it. The imitative power of several species of the corous and psittacus kinds is well known ; the jay, and parrot, are those most commonly taught, and the far-famed parrot of the late Colonel O'Kelly which could repeat twenty of our most popular songs, and sing them to their proper tunes, has been, I suppose, seen and heard by many.

The Bullfinch (Coxia Pyrrhula) however, has a better voice, as well as a more correct taste in imitating musical tones, and the bird breeders of Germany find a lucrative employment in training multitudes of this family for a foreign market. There is no species, however, so much entitled to notice on account of its voice, as the Polyglottis, or Mocking-Bird of South Carolina. This is an individual of the Thrush kind ; its own natural note is delightfully musical and solemn ; but beyond this it possesses an instinctive talent of imitating the note of every other kind of singing bird, and even the voice of every bird of prey so exactly, as to deceive the very kind it attempts to mock. It is moreover playful enough to find amusement in the deception ; and takes a pleasure in decoying smaller birds near it by imitating their notes, when it frightens them almost to death, or drives them away with all speed, by pouring upon them the screams of such birds of prey as they dread.

Now it is clear that the imitative, like the natural voice, has its seat in the cartilages and other moveable powers that form the Larynx: for the great body of the trachea only gives measure to the sound, and renders it more or less copious in proportion to its volume. It is not, therefore, to be wondered at, that a similar sort of imitative power should be sometimes cultivated with success in the human larynx; and that we should occasionally meet with persons, who from long and dexterous practice, should be able to imitate the notes of almost all the singing birds of the woods, or the sounds of other animals, or even to personate the different voices of orators and other public speakers.

VENTRILOQUISM is the power of imitating voices, sounds, or noises, as if they were perfectly extraneous, and not originating in the utterer, but in some other person, and in places at various distances, and even in several directions. A skillful ventriloquist produces these effects without any apparent movement of his jaws, lips, or features. Various opinions have been advanced by physiologists with regard to the manner of producing such an effect. The most commonly recorded opinion refers to the power of articulation during inspiration. M. Majendia regards it as a mere modification of the ordinary voice, so as to imitate the sounds which the voice suffers from distance; and lately Müller contends that, it "consists in inspiring deeply, so as to protrude forward the abdominal viscera by the distent of the diaphragm, and then speaking while the expiration is performed very slowly through a very narrow glottis by means of the sides of the chest alone, the diaphragm maintaining its depressed position. Sounds may be thus uttered which resemble the voice of a person calling from a distance." This· is a very probable explanation, especially as the imagination influences the judgment when we direct the ear to the place whence the ventriloquist pretends that the sound proceeds : a part of the trick which is always taken advantage of by the ventriloquist.

The art of ventriloquism was known at a very early period and was generally regarded by the ignorant as a supernatural gift, associated with sorcery. It was one of the evidences against a person accused of sorcery, and of course had a share in producing their condemnation. In the seventeenth century a woman named Cecele astonished the inhabitants of Lisbon with her powers as a ventriloquist; she was convicted of being a sorceress, and possessed of a demon ; and, although she was not burned, yet, she was transported to the island of St. Thomas, where she died.

The influence of ventriloquism over the human race is not, therefore, wonderful, when we preceive that it is not merely confined to the imitation of sounds and voices on earth, but that he has, in a certain degree, the supernatural at command. The power which it must have given to the pagan priesthood, in addition to their other deceptions may be imagined.

ILLUSION OF SOUND.

THE ear is the most fertile source of our illusions and the ancient magicians seem to have been very successful in turning to their purposes the doctrines of sound. In the labyrinth of Egypt, which contained twelve places and 1500 subterraneous apartments, the gods were made to speak in a voice of thunder ; and Pliny, in whose time this singular structure existed, informs us that some of the palaces were so constructed that their doors could not be opened without permitting peals of thunder from being heard in the interior. When Darius Hystaspes ascended the throne, and allowed his subjects to prostrate themselves before him as a god, of the divinity of his character was impressed upon his worshippers by the bursts of thunder and flashes of lightning which accompanied their devotion. History has of course, not informed us how these effects were produced ; but it is probable, that in the subterraneous and vaulted apartments of the Egyptian labyrinth, the reverberated sounds arising from the mere opening and shutting of the doors themselves afforded a sufficient imitation of ordinary thunder. In the palace of the Persian King, however, a more artificial imitation is likely to be employed, and it is not improbable that the method used in our modern theatres was known to the ancients. A thin sheet of iron, three or four feet long, such as that used for German stoves, is held by one corner between the finger and the thumb, and allowed to hang freely by its own weight. The hand is then moved or shaken horizontally, so as to agitate the corner in a direction at right angles to the surface of the sheet. By this simple process a great variety of sounds, will be produced, varying from the deep growl of distant thunder to those loud and explosive bursts which rattle in quick succession from clouds immediately over our heads.   The operator soon acquires great power over this instrument, so as to be able to produce from it any intensity and character of sound that may be required.   The same effect may be produced by sheets of tin-plate, and by thin plates of mica ; but on account of their small size, the sound is shorter and more acute.   In modern exhibitions an admirable imitation of lightning is produced by throwing the powder of rosin, or the dust of lycopodium, through a flame, and the rattling showers of rain which accompany these meteors are well imitated by a well regulated shower of peas.

The principal pieces of acoustic mechanism used by the ancients were *speaking or singing heads*, which were constructed for the purpose of representing the gods, or of uttering oracular responses.   Among these, the speaking head of Orpheus, which uttered its responses at Lesbos, is one of the most famous.   It was celebrated, not only throughout Greece, but even in Persia, and it had the credit of predicting, in the equivocal language of the heathen oracles, the bloody death which terminated the expiation of Cyrus the Great in Scythia.   Odin, the mighty magician of the North, who imported into Scandinavia the magical arts of the East, possessed a speaking head, said to be that of the sage Minos, which he had encased in gold, and which uttered responses that had all the authority of a divine revelation.

The celebrated mechanic Gerbert, who filled the

papal chair A. D. 1000, under the name of Sylvester
II. constructed a speaking head of brass. Albertus
Magmus is said to have executéd a head in the thirteenth century, which not only moved but spoke. It
was made of earthenware, and Thomas Aquinas is
said to have been so *terrified* when he saw it, that he
broke it in pieces, upon which the mechanist exclaimed,
" There goes the labor of thirty years. "

It has been supposed by some authors, that in the
ancient speaking machines the deception is effected by
means of ventriloquism, the voice issuing from the
juggler himself; but it is more probable that the sound
was conveyed by pipes from a person in another apartment to the mouth of the figure. Lucian, indeed,
expressly informs us, that the impostor Alexander
made his figure of Æsculapius speak by transmitting
his voice through the gullet of a crane to the mouth
of his statue ; and that this method was general appears from a passage in Theodoretus, who assures
us, that in the fourth century, when Bishop Theophilus
broke to pieces the statues at Alexandria, he found
some which were hollow, and which were so placed
against a wall that the priest could conceal himself
behind them, and addresses the ignorant spectators
through their mouths.

Even in modern times, speaking machines have been
constructed on this principle. The figure is frequently
a mere head placed upon a hollow pedestal, which, in
order to promote the deception, contains a pair of
bellows, a sounding board, a cylinder and pipes supposed to represent the organs of speech. In other
cases, these are dispensed with, and a simple wooden

head utters its sounds through a speaking trumpet. At the court of Charles II. this deception was exhibited with great effect by one Thomas Irson, an Englishman, and when the astonishment had become general, a popish priest was discovered by one of the pages in an adjoining apartment. The questions had been proposed to the wooden figure by whispering into its ear, and this learned personage had answered them all with great ability, by speaking through a pipe in the same language in which the questions were proposed.

Although the performances of speaking heads were effected by the method now described, yet there is reason to think that the ventriloquist sometimes presided at the exhibition and deceived the audience by his extraordinary powers of illusion. There is no species of deception more irresistable in its effects, than that which arises from the uncertainty with which we judge of the direction and distance of sounds. Every person must have noticed how a sound in their own ears is often mistaking for some loud noise moderated by the distance from which it is supposed to come; and the sportsman must have frequently been surprised at the existence of musical sounds humming remotely in the extended heath, when it was only the wind sounding in the barrel of his gun. The great proportion of apparitions that haunt old castles and apartments associated with death exist only in the sounds which accompany them. The imagination even of the boldest inmate of a place hallowed by superstition will transfer some trifling sound near his own person to a direction and to a distance very different from the truth, and the sound, which otherwise might have no

peculiar complexion, will deceive another character
from its new locality.   Spurning the idea of a supernatural origin, he determines to unmask the sceptre,
and grapple with it in its den.   All the inmates of the
house are found to be asleep, even the quadrupeds are
in their lair ; there is not a breath of wind to ruffle the
lake that reflects through the casements the reclining
crescent of the night ; and the massive walls in which
he is enclosed forbid the idea that he has been disturbed
by the warping of paneling or the bending of partitions.
His search is vain : and he remains master of his own
secret till he has another opportunity of investigation.
The same sound again disturbs him, and, modified
probably by his own position at the time, it may perhaps appear to come in a direction slightly different
from the last.   His searches are resumed, and he is
again disappointed.   If this incident should recur night
after night with the same result ; if the sound should
appear to depend upon his own motions, or be any how
associated with himself, with his present feelings or
with his past .history, his personal courage will give
way, a superstitious dread, at which he himself perhaps
laughs, will seize his mind, and he would rather believe
that the sounds have a supernatural origin than that
they could continue to issue from a spot where he
knows there is no natural cause for their production.

I have had occasion to have personal knowledge of
a case much stronger than that which has now been
put.   A gentleman devoid of all superstitious feelings,
and living in a house free from any gloomy associations,
heard night after night in his bedroom a singular noise,

unlike any ordinary sound to which he was accustomed.
He had slept in the same room for years without
hearing it, and he attributed it at first to some change
of circumstances in the roof or in the walls of the room,
but after the strictest examination, no cause could be
found for it.   It occurred only once in the night : it
was heard almost every night ; with few interruptions.
It was over in an instant, and never took place till after
the gentleman had gone to bed.   It was always distinctly heard by his companion, to whose time of going
to bed it had no relation.   It depended upon the gentleman alone, and it followed him into another apartment
with another bed, on the opposite side of the house.
Accustomed to such investigations, he made the most
diligent but fruitless search into its cause.   The con-
sideration that the sound had a special reference to
him alone operated upon his imagination, and he did
not scruple to acknowledge that the recurrence of the
mysterious sound produced a superstitious feeling at
the moment.   Many months afterwards it was found
that the sound arose from the partial opening of the
door of a wardrobe which was within a few feet of the
gentleman's head, and which had been taken into the
other apartment.   This wardrobe was almost always
opened before he retired to bed, and the door being a
little too tight, it gradually forced itself open with a
sort of dull sound resembling the note of a drum.   As
the door had only started half an inch out of its place,
its change of place never attracted attention.   The
sound indeed, seemed to come in a different direction,
and from a greater distance.

The uncertainty with respect to the direction of sound is the foundation of the art of ventriloquism. If we place ten men in a row at such a distance from us that they are included in the angle within which we cannot judge of the direction of sound, and if in a calm day each of them speaks in succession, we shall not be able with closed eyes to determine from which of the ten men any of the sounds proceeds, and we shall be incapable of perceiving that there is any difference in the direction of the sounds emitted by the two outer-most. If a man and a child are placed within the same angle, and if the man speaks with the accent of a child without any corresponding motion in his mouth or face, we shall necessarily believe that the voice comes from the child : nay, if the child is so distant from the man that the voice actually appears to us to come from the man, we will still continue in belief that the child is the speaker; and the conviction would acquire additional strength if the child favored the deception by accommodating its features and gestures to the words spoken by the man. So powerful, indeed, is the influence of this deception, that if a jackass placed near the man were to open its mouth, and shake its head responsive to the words uttered by his neighbor, we would rather believe that the ass spoke than that the sounds proceeded from a person whose mouth was shut, and the muscles of whose face were in perfect repose. If our imagination were even directed to a marble statue or a lump of inanimate matter, as the source from which we were to expect the sounds to issue, we would still be deceived, and would refer the

sounds even to these lifeless objects.   The illusion
would be greatly promoted if the voice were totally
different in its tone and character from that of the man
from whom it really comes ; and if he occasionally
spoke in his own full and measured voice, the belief
will be irresistible that the assumed voice proceeds from
the quadruped or from the inanimate object.

When the sounds which are required to proceed from
any given object are such as they are actually calculated to yield, the process of deception is extremely easy,
and it may be successfully executed even if the angle
between the real and the supposed directions of the
sound is much greater than the angle of uncertainty.
Mr. Dugald Stewart has stated some cases in which
deceptions of this kind were very perfect.   He mentions his having seen a person who, by counterfeiting
the gesticulations of a performer on the violin, while
he imitated the music by his voice, riveted the eyes of
his audience on the instrument, though every sound
they heard was produced from his own mouth.   The late
Savile Carey, who imitated the whistling of the wind
through a narrow chink, told Mr. Stewart that he had
frequently practised this deception in the corner of a
coffee-house, and that he seldom failed to see some of
the company rise to examine the tightness of the win-
dows, while others, more intent on their newspapers,
contented themselves with putting on their hats and
buttoning their coats.   Mr. Stewart likewise mentions
an exhibition formerly common in some of the con-
tinental theatres, where a performer on the stage dis-
played the dumb show of singing with his lips and eyes
and gestures, while another person unseen supplied the

music with his voice.   The deception in this case he found to be at first so complete as to impose upon the nicest ear and the quickest eye ; but in the progress of the entertainment, he became distinctly sensible of the imposition, and sometimes wondered that it should have misled him for a moment.   In this case there can be no doubt that the deception was at first the work of the imagination, and was not sustained by the acoustic principle.   The real and the mock singer were too distant, and when the influence of the imagination subsided, the true direction of the sound was discovered. This detection of the imposture, however, may have arisen from another cause.   If the mock singer happened to change the position of his head, while the real singer made no corresponding change in his voice, the attentive spectator would at once notice this incongruity, and discover the imposition.

In many of the feats of ventriloquism the performer contrives, under some pretence or other, to conceal his face, but ventriloquists of great distinction, such as M. Alexandre, practice their art without any such concealment.

Ventriloquism loses its distinctive character if its imitations are not performed by a voice from the belly. The voice, indeed, does not actually come from that region, but when the ventriloquist utters sounds from the larynx without moving the muscles of his face, he gives them strength by a powerful action of the abdominal muscles.   Hence he speaks by means of his belly, although the throat is the real source from which the ʻsounds proceed.   Mr. Dugald Stewart has doubted the fact that ventriloquists possess the power of fetching a voice from within : he cannot conceive what aid could be derived from such an extraordinary power ; and he considers that the imagination, when seconded by such powers of imitation as some mimics possess, is quite sufficient to account for all the phenomena of ventrilo- quism which he has heard.   The opinion, however, is strongly opposed by the remark made to Mr. Stewart himself by a ventriloquist, " that his art would be per- fect if it were possible only to speak distinctly, without any movement of the lips at all."   But, independent of this admission, it is a matter of absolute certainty that this internal power is exercised by the true ventriloquist. In the account which the Abbe Chapelle has given of the performances of M. St. Gille and Louis Brabant, he distinctly states that M. St. Gille appeared to be absolutely mute while he was exercising his art, and that no change in his countenance could be discovered.* He affirms also that the countenance of Louis Brabant exhibited no change, and that his lips were close and inactive.   M. Richerand, who attentively watched the performances of M. Fitz-James, assures us that during his exhibition there was a distension in the epigastric region, and that he could not long continue the exertion without fatigue.

The influence over the human mind which the ven- triloquist derives from the skilful practice of his art, is greater than that which is exercised by any other spe- cies of conjurer.   The ordinary magician requires his theatre, his accomplices, and the instruments of his art, and he enjoys but a local sovereignty within the pre- cincts of his own magic circle.   The ventriloquist, on

---

* Edinburgh Journal of Science, No. xviii. p. 254.

E

the contrary, has the supernatural always at his command. In the open fields, as well as in the crowded
city—in the private apartment, as well as in the public
hall, he can summon up innumerable spirits ; and though
the persons of his fictitious dialogue are not visible to
the eye, yet they are as unequivocally present to the
imagination of his auditors as if they had been shad-
owed forth in the silence of a spectral form. In order
to convey some idea of the influence of this illusion, I
shall mention a few well authenticated cases of successful
ventriloquism.

M. St. Gille, a grocer of St. Germain en Laye, whose
performances have been recorded by the Abbe de la
Chapelle, had occasion to shelter himself from a storm
in a neighboring convent, where the monks were in
deep mourning for a much-esteemed member of their
community who had been recently buried. While
lamenting over the tomb of their deceased brother the
slight honors which had been paid to his memory, a
voice was suddenly heard to issue from the roof of the
choir bewailing the condition of the deceased in purgatory, and reproving the brotherhood for their want of
zeal. The tidings of this supernatural event brought
the whole brotherhood to the church. The voice from
above repeated its lamentations and reproaches, and
the whole convent fell upon their faces, and vowed to
make a reparation of the error. They accordingly
chaunted in full choir a *de profundis*, during the
intervals of which the spirit of the departed monk
expressed his satisfaction at their pious exercises. The
prior afterward inveighed against modern skepticism
on the subject of apparitions, and M. St. Gille had great

difficulty in convincing the fraternity that the whole was a deception.

On another occasion, a commission of the Royal Academy of Sciences at Paris, attended by several persons of the highest rank, met at St. Germain en Laye to witness the performances of M. St. Gille. The real object of this meeting was purposely withheld from a lady of the party, who was informed that an aerial spirit had lately established itself in the neighborhood, and that the object of the assembly was to investigate the matter. When the party had sat down to dinner in the open air, the spirit addressed the lady in a voice which seemed to come from above their heads, from the surface of the ground at a great distance, or from a considerable depth under her feet. Having been thus addressed at intervals during two hours, the lady was firmly convinced of the existence of the spirit, and could with difficulty be undeceived.

Another ventriloquist, Louis Brabant, who had been valet-de-chambre to Francis I., turned his powers to a more profitable account. Having fallen in love with a rich and beautiful heiress, he was rejected by her parents as an unsuitable match for their daughter. On the death of her father, Louis paid a visit to the widow, and he had no sooner entered the house than she heard the voice of her deceased husband addressing her from above : " Give my daughter in marriage to Louis Brabant, who is a man of large fortune and excellent character. I endure the inexpressible torments of purgatory for having refused her to him. Obey this admonition, and give everlasting repose to the soul of your poor husband." This awful command could not be resisted, and the widow announced her compliance with it.

As our conjuror, however, required money for the completion of his marriage, he resolved to work upon the fears of one Cornu, an old banker at Lyons, who had amassed immense wealth by usury and extortion. Having obtained an interview with the miser, he introduced the subjects of demons and spectres and the torments of purgatory; and during an interval of silence, the voice of the miser's deceased father was heard complaining of his dreadful situation in purgatory, and calling upon his son to rescue him from his sufferings, by enabling Louis Brabant to redeem the Christians that were enslaved by the Turks. The awe-struck miser was also threatened with eternal damnation if he did not thus expiate his own sins; but such was the grasp that the banker took of his gold, that the ventriloquist was obliged to pay him another visit. On this occasion, not only his father but all his deceased relations appealed to him in behalf of his own soul and theirs, and such was the loudness of their complaints that the spirit of the banker was subdued, and he gave the ventriloquist ten thousand crowns to liberate the Christian captives. When the miser was afterward undeceived, he is said to have been so mortified that he died of vexation.

The ventriloquists of the nineteenth century made great additions to their art, and the performances of M. Fitz-James and M. Alexandre, which must have been seen by many of our countrymen, were far superior to those of their predecessors. Besides the art of speaking by the muscles of the throat and the abdomen,

without moving those of the face, these artists had not
only studied with great diligence and success the modi-
fications which sounds of all kinds undergo from distance, obstructions, and other causes, but had acquired
the art of imitating them in the highest perfection.
The ventriloquist was therefore able to carry on a
dialogue in which the *dramatis voces*, as they may be
called, were numerous ; and when on the outside of an
apartment he could personate a mob with its infinite
variety of noise and vociferation.   Their influence over
an audience was still further extended by a singular
power over the muscles of the body.   M. Fitz-James
actually succeeded in making the opposite or corresponding muscles act differently from each other ;
and while one side of his face was merry and laughing,
the other was full of sorrow and in tears.   At one
moment he was tall, thin, and melancholic ; and after
passing behind a screen, he came out "bloated with
obesity and staggering with fulness."   M. Alexandre
possessed the same power over his face and figure, and
so striking was the contrast of two of these forms, that
an excellent sculptor, Mr. Joseph, has perpetuated
them in marble.

This new acquirement of the ventriloquist enabled
him, in his own single person, and with his own single
voice, to represent upon the stage a dramatic com-
position which would have required the assistance of
several actors.   Although only one character in the
piece could be seen at the same time, yet they all appeared during its performance, and the change of the
face and figure on the part of the ventriloquist was so
perfect that his personal identity could not be recognised

in the *dramatis personæ*.   This deception was rendered
still more complete by a particular construction of the
dresses, which enabled the performer to re-appear
in a new character after an interval so short that
the audience necessarily believed that it was another
person.

It is a curious circumstance that Captain Lyon found
among the Eskimaux of Igloolik ventriloquists of no
mean skill.   There is much rivalry among the professors
of the art, who do not expose each other's secrets, and
their exhibitions derive great importance from the rarity
of their occurrence.   The following account of one of
them is so interesting, that we shall give the whole of
it in Captain Lyon's words.

" Among our Igloolik acquaintances were two females
and a few male wizards, of whom the principal was
Toolemak.   This personage was cunning and intelligent,
and, whether professionally, or from his skill in the
chase, but perhaps from both reasons, was considered
by all the tribe as a man of importance.   As I inva-
riably paid great deference to his opinion on all subjects
connected with his calling, he freely communicated to
me his superior knowledge, and did not scruple to
allow of my being present at his interviews with Tornga,
or his patron spirit.   In consequence of this, I took
an early opportunity of requesting my friend to exhibit
his skill in my cabin.   His old wife was with him, and
by much flattery and an accidental display of a glitter-
ing knife and some beads, she assisted me in obtaining
my request.   All light excluded, our sorcerer began
chaunting to his wife with great vehemence, and she
in return answered by singing the Amna-aya, which

was not discontinued during the whole ceremony. As far as I could hear, he afterward began turning himself rapidly around, and in a loud, powerful voice, vociferated for Tornga with great impatience, at the same time blowing and snorting like a walrus. His noise, impatience, and agitation, increased every moment, and he at length seated himself on the deck, varying his tones, and making a rustling with his clothes. Suddenly the voice seemed smothered, and was so managed as to sound as if retreating beneath the deck, each moment becoming more distant, and ultimately giving the idea of being many feet below the cabin, when it ceased entirely. His wife now, in answer to my queries, informed me very seriously, that he had dived, and that he would send up Tornga. Accordingly, in about half a minute, a distant blowing was heard very slowly approaching, and a voice, which differed from that at first heard, was at times mingled with the blowing, until at length both sounds became distinct, and the old woman informed me that Tornga was come to answer my questions. I accordingly asked several questions of the sagacious spirit, to each of which inquiries I received an answer by two loud claps on the deck, which I was given to understand were favorable.

"A very hollow yet powerful voice, certainly much different from the tones of Toolemak, now chanted for some time, and a strange jumble of hisses, groans, shouts, and gabblings like a turkey, succeeded in rapid order. The old woman sang with increased energy, and as I took it for granted that this was all intended to astonish the Kabloona, I cried repeatedly that I

was very much afraid.   This, as I expected, added
fuel to the fire, until the poor immortal, exhausted by
its own might, asked leave to retire.

"The voice gradually sank from our hearing as at
first, and a very indistinct hissing succeeded ; in its
advance, it sounded like the tone produced by the wind
on the bass chord of an Æolian harp.   This was soon
changed to a rapid hiss like that of a rocket, and
Toolemak with a yell announced his return.   I had
held my breath at the first distant hissing, and twice
exhausted myself ; yet our conjurer did not once respire,
and even his returning and powerful yell was uttered
without a previous stop or inspiration of air.

"Light being admitted, our wizard, as might be
expected, was in a profouse perspiration, and certainly
much exhausted by his exertions, which had continued
for at least half an hour.   We now observed a couple
of bunches, each consisting of two strips of white deer-
skin and a long piece of sinew, attached to the back of
his coat.   These we had not seen before, and were
informed that they had been sewn on by Tornga while
he was below." *

Captain Lyon had the good fortune to witness
another of Toolemak's exhibitions, and he was much
struck with the wonderful steadiness of the wizard
throughout the whole performance, which lasted an
hour and a half.   He did not once appear to move, for
he was close to the skin behind which Captain Lyon
did not hear the least rustling of his clothes, or even

---

* Private Journal of Captain G. F. Lyon.   Lond. 1824,
p. 358, 361.

distinguish his breathing, although his outcries were made with great exertion.

The following is a description of Ventriloqual exercises performed by Professor Wyman: in which he explains the finesse and manner of placing the muscles of the throat and tongue.

THE SPEAKING AUTOMATA, IN IMITATION OF THE

ROMAN ORACLES.

THE first introduction of a speaking automata took place in the last century. It was the image of a body, and performed by a Spanish Count for the amusement of his visitors. An Automata was introduced into England some fifty years since, by a person with a wooden leg, and who for the exhibition of this figure alone received twenty pounds sterling a week. Mr. Mathews the accomplished commedian also introduced in one of his popular entertainments a speaking Tommy, as he called it. His performance of which did not add fresh laurels to his fame. It was from that gentleman I took the idea of introducing in my entertainment a speaking automata.

The figure, when performed without the operator moving his lips—and holding a lighted candle to his mouth when the figure appears to speak—and appearing to drink also—is a pleasing and extraordinary piece of vocal deception as can be practised. The imagination of the spectators is doubly kept in play, for they have the object before them, and the deception is so well kept up when the figure is made to move its lips, that repetitions of it, however numerous, are always amusing.

The lips of my automaton are made to move by a small spring which I touch (when he appears to speak,) with the fore-finger of the right hand, the figure being held by the waist with the other fingers and thumb. The tone of the voice used for the figure can only be acquired by practice. It is not a natural tone, and as such must be found out by the practitioner in regulating the ventricles of the larynx, those of pain and the falsetto voice being produced altogether in that part. To keep the lips from moving the teeth must be compressed together, which keep the muscles of the face and lips from vibrating, but it is impossible for the letters B, M, P, to be articulated distinctly. The conversation must be adapted expressly for the figures when the letters B, M, and P, are seldom or never used. It is impossible for any man to speak and drink at the same time, although I always give such appearances that no one (but a person thoroughly acquainted with the anatomy of the throat,) would credit but that I did. The opening of the vinea-glottdus, (the chink by which we breathe,) which as it is narrower or wider modulates and tunes the voice ; is so exquisitely moved by its muscles, and so spasmodically shut when it is touched by a drop of water or a crumb of bread, that the valve of the glottis or the epi-glottis standing over it, flaps down like the key of a wind instrument, so that it is utterly impossible for any one to both articulate and drink at the same time ; the best attempt to draw the breath while swallowing will produce an accident.

In making the figure appear to speak during the time a lighted candle is held close to my lips, I need only add, that the quantity of air requisite to articulate

cr form the tone of the voice for the figure is so small
that there is not sufficient force of air to move the
flame in the least.

To bring this feat of ventriloquism to the perfection
of deceiving all beholders, a constant and unlimited
practice of years is necessary. The quickest trans-
action of the performers voice from the figures to his
own, will take months of practise alone. The least
mistake arising from the change of the voice, the spell
is lost, and the operator may return his automaton to
his chest till he gets fresh spectators.

In the imitation of voices of adults, the contraction
of the thyro-arytenoid muscles are used to increase or
diminish the production of grouse or acute sounds, the
contraction of these muscles, closes in part, the glottis,
particularly the anterior half, the elongation or decura-
tion of the trachea or portevent will occasion mortifi-
cation. Also raising or depressing the velum palati
will make the voice nearer or more remote, at the
pleasure of the operator. When I introduce a gruff
old man's voice, and want to make it appear at a distance, I compress the tongue as if in the act of swallowing; the ary-tenoid cartilages will then touch at
their inner surfaces; it is then I speak, (articulating
with the tongue, shaped like a spoon, and in a per-
pendicular position in the mouth) that the voice will
have a grave, hollow, and smothered tone. The imagination of the spectators having previously been down
to the place where the supposed person is, and the voice
so beautifully regulated as to imitate and be in unison
of the same tone as a natural voice in the same place
would be, the deception will be complete. The imagi-

nation, is quite sufficient to account for all the phenomena of ventriloquism. In bringing the voice nearer,
the tongue must be gradually brought to its proper
position ; the effect of which will lessen the contraction
of the thyro-ary-tenoid muscles ; the voice will naturally
grow more clear and louder as the contraction decreases.
The vibration of the above muscles produce the vocal
sound. In the production of the above voices there
is a great distention in the epigastric region, that makes
it impossible to continue the exertion long without
fatigue. Indeed such is the exertion to produce the
voice of a person at a distance, (the muscles of the
throat and abdomen being in a state of severe contraction,) that it is my firm opinion that no one could speak
thirty seconds, and not change the tone of his voice
without breaking a blood-vessel.

But the natural voice of the practitioner in answering
or asking questions of the supposed person obviates
this inconvenience. It is in changing the natural voice
so suddenly into the artificial that requires such immense
practice and study. The novelty of asking and having
to answer the different questions is of itself a task not
very soon got over. Reader when you hear me ask in
my own natural voice for a bottle of wine of a supposed
person in the cellar—the whole of the abdominal with
fifteen pair of muscles belonging to the throat have
instantly to be contracted for the simple answer of
'what do you want ?' And when the voice approaches
nearer, the contraction must be regulated that the voice
appears to approach without the least motion of my
lips or body. In fact the operator's situation is any-
thing but agreeable ; having to compose the dialogue

—ask and answer the different questions—regulate the tension of the voice—and, for every sentence uttered by the supposed person, to contract the muscles of the throat and abdomen.

Mimicry, or imitation of various animals and instruments is possessed by many ; indeed I have met several persons who could imitate noises which I found by reputed practice impossible for me to attain. The barking of a dog is produced by the breath of inspiration ; the growl is produced by placing the tongue close to the roof of the mouth, and the bark by suddenly placing the tongue in its proper place, lets the air have a sudden and free egress into the lungs. This noise, viz : barking, is modulated by the rising or depressing the velum palate. The grunting of the pig is occasioned in the same manner, viz : by inspiration, but the air drawn into the lungs is made to pass chiefly through the nostrils. The noise—hume—is produced by the air through the nostrils, and the squeak—whee—through the mouth, with the tongue in its proper position. The neighing of a foal is also imitated by the air of inspiration. Several imitations of animals besides those already mentioned, take place during inspiration ; but the old hypotheses of the ventriloquist speaking while the breath is passing into the lungs and not from them, is false ; it is virtually impossible to utter any articulated sound, by the breath of inspiration, so as to be called articulate language. Let any person say the words *hume, whee,* during the inspiration of the breath, and he will find that instead of saying the words distinctly, so as to be understood, that he will give a pretty fair imitation of the pig. The buzzing of the fly may be produced by placing the upper lip about half an inch over the lower lip, and blowing the air between them. The crying of a child is produced by a small quill being cut at one end when you commence to make a pen the first cut must be drawn near to the end but not entirely off, then cut the quill or tube from the stalk, place the end in the mouth that is cut, blow down it and it will produce a squeaking sound similar to a child crying ; this is modulated by the hand covering, or partially covering the open end of the quill. The common method of imitating birds is produced by the common bird call, used by many sportsmen ; a piece of tin perfectly round, the shape or size of a dollar, is bent so as to produce half a circle ; in the centre of the flat end is punched a hole large enough for three pins to be placed in ; this being placed in the mouth, the round edges between the lips, will produce a whistle similar to several birds.

I respectfully acquaint the reader that I do not use one of these instruments. The din of expiration passed through the nose during the mechanical raising and falling of the larynx, will regulate the size of the aperture of the glottis, which notes may then be produced by close attention to a most fatiguing practice. The imitation of the same is produced by making a noise similar to hawking, viz : if a person will place his tongue in the same position as he does when hawking previous to spitting, and modulate the tone of the noise so caused, which noise must be produced by both the air of inspiration and expiration, he will have a good imitation of the carpenters' saw. The plane is imitated in a similar manner, only it requires more modulation. False ventriloquism or false modulation of the voice, is produced by the common hat which the operator wears. Let him place himself in a closet in his own house out of the view of the audience—then suppose that in this closet there are stairs that lead to the rooms below—let him call loud for any person— for instance, he says, who is down there ? he must then place his hat over his face which will . completely smother his voice, which must be an imitation of some one, not his own natural voice. He must then answer with the hat compressed to his face—the answer of the supposed person. The voice .of the supposed person is made to appear nearer by taking the hat gradually from the face,—the closer the hat is compressed the farther off will the voice appear, if well managed by the operator in keeping the imagination of his audience in good play. This is the difference between real and artificial modulation of the voice. A clever ventrilo- quist or vocal modulator is able to converse before his audience and modulate his voice without moving the muscles of his face ; whereas merely a mimic will pass himself off as a ventriloquist or vocal modulator, by keeping his person invisible.

SECOND SIGHT MYSTERY.

As a great deal of anxiety has been manifested in every part of the community respecting this very suc- cessful and ingenious method of silent telegraphing, or, in other terms, the. phenomena of SECOND SIGHT, or seeing without eyes, and by many called, " Clairvoyance," for this reason I feel it my duty, as well as a gratification to myself and others, to make some comment upon the subject, together with a brief explanation of the manner in which it may be performed.

When the "SECOND SIGHT *Mystery*" was first introduced, it was not intended for a speculative trick, or to be introduced before the fashionable assemblages of our theatres, museums, and public places of amusement, but was simply designed for the social circle and fireside amusement. We could scarcely conceive of a more pleasant yet innocent recreation than that of the present method of seeing, as it were, without the use of our eyes. One of the party being brought forward, and carefully blindfolded, or even placed in an adjoining room, may readily conceive the name and description of every article held in the hands of the opposite party, without the least recourse or bribery or accomplicy. We are well aware that even all the principal tricks of jugglers, magicians, &c., as practiced at present, are accomplished by means of collusion through a third person. But in the present no such recourse is necessary, as any two persons, by committing to memory the following examples, are enabled to perform the experiment of second sight. I am well satisfied that there are at present numerous professors of mesmerism and pretended clairvoyants who are continually impressing upon the minds of the public that they, the clairvoyants, are enabled, through the medium of electro or animal magnetism, to distinguish and describe *foreign lands*, hidden treasures, and even to tell the thoughts of those whom they never seen, and could not have had any correspondence whatever.

All this *they profess* to do without any recourse to bribery or the optical vision.

This illusion they have carried very successful for a number of years, and in fact the community never recognized the second sight under any other circumstances than when connected with demonstrations of their so-called clairvoyance. I have frequently, when exhibiting this experiment in various parts of the country, been very much annoyed by sudden contentions arising out of inconceivable ideas respecting the manner of correspondence.

One says it is clairvoyance, another mesmerism, or psychology : some say it is a spiritual manifestation, others say ventriloquism. Thus we see many ideas advanced by many different people ; yet all are totally ignorant of the true method of its accomplishment. A careful perusal of the following book will scatter every erroneous idea concerning the supposed miracle. This beautiful trick has progressed rapidly from its infancy, and was for a great length of time withheld from the criticism of the public, and only exhibited in private circles, but recently it has acquired a considerable popularity, and is now daily astonishing the multitudes who witness its demonstrations with wonder and delight.

NOTICE.

THE science of " Second Sight " teaches any person the true method by which they are enabled, through the medium of SOUND, to distinguish the *color, name,* and *quality* of any articles that may be held in the hands of an operator. Also, to tell the *number, dates, quantity, time, direction,* &c., during which time the subject may be satisfactorily blindfolded, or even placed in some other apartment, will readily describe all the above-named *orders* to which it belongs, thus making it a highly interesting exhibition of ingenuity and talent. It is not expected, however, that every person who reads this little book intends putting the examples into practice, but the reading of it once through is well worth the price asked for it, and a gratification to know that the "secret is out."

CLAIRVOYANCE EXPOSED;

OR, THE SECOND-SIGHT MYSTERY.

AS PERFORMED ORIGINALLY BY MRS. HANNINGTON, PROFESSOR WYMAN, ROBERT HELLER, AND MRS. LOOMIS,

LESSON I.

NOTE.—Great care should be taken by the operator not to PLACE the *least stress* or to *emphasize* upon any *letter, word,* or *sound.* Speak natural, loud, and distinct, in order that the subject may hear with accuracy every sound that is uttered. The subject must also speak loud and distinct, so that the audience may hear every answer clearly. All the CUES in this science are *thus,* and must be impressed upon the mind of both the subject and the operator, but not regarded in any example of communication.

A correct distinction of all COLORS may be known by the following examples :—

EXAMPLE I.

What color? White.
What *is the* color? Black.

What color *is this?*   Red.

Name the color ?   Blue.

Describe the color ?   Green.

Can you tell the color of this, that, or them ? Yellow.

What is color as *near as you can tell?*   Brown.

What is color of the *article?*   Gray.

Tell me what color, &c. ?   Mixed.

EXAMPLE II.

Tell me the color of *this* handkerchief?   Mixed colors; and RED the most prominent color, &c.

NOTE.—The best method to distinguish any variety of mixed colors is first to distinguish the most prominent color of the article by first asking any one of the above direct questions denoting its most prominent color, and immediately after the answer is given it should be repeated thus :

Describe the color?   Green. Repeat Green ? Yes, a variety of mixed colors, but green is the most prominent.

Thus all mixed colors may be known in a corresponding manner.

LESSON II.

TABLE OF NUMERALS.

What Number of any article	Denotes	1
What *is the* Number of any article	"	2
What Number can you *see* of any article	"	3
What Number can you *tell* of any article	"	4
Count the Number of any article	"	5

Please to count the number signifies that more than five are to be enumerated when the signal bell may be

acceded to, and subject commences to count slowly the
number specified.   Thus :

								Ring.	2	3	4	5	6
							1	2	"	3	4	5	6	7
						1	2	3	"	4	5	6	7	8
					1	2	3	4	"	5	6	7	8	9
				1	2	3	4	5	"	6	7	8	9	10
			1	2	3	4	5	6	"	7	8	9	10	11
		1	2	3	4	5	6	7	"	8	9	10	11	12
	1	2	3	4	5	6	7	8	"	9	10	11	12	13
1	2	3	4	5	6	7	8	9	"	10	11	12	13	14
1 2 3 4 5 6 7 8 9 10									"	11	12	13	14	15

The above is only a fac-simile of the ordinary addi-
tion-table, (as 1 and 5 are 6, or 10 and 5 are 15,) the
highest number being the one thought of.   It would
not be appropriate to adopt this principle to enumerate
more than 25, as it becomes tedious to calculate so
slowly in order to arrive at the intended number ; consequently I have annexed a few simple questions to
denote any number more than 25, or less than 100.
Thus :

LESSON III.

	Ring	30
What Number of any article, and		
Repeat " " "	"	35
What *is the* Number of any article, and	"	40
Repeat " " "	"	45
What Number can you *see* of any article, and	"	50
Repeat " " "	"	55
What Number can you *tell* of any article, and	"	60
Repeat " " " "	"	65
Count the Number of any article, and	"	70
Repeat " " "	"	75

Tell me the Number of any article, and   " 80
    Repeat   "   "   "   " 85
Please to count the Number of any article, and " 90
    Repeat   "   "   "   " 95
What three figures denote the number   " 100

NOTE. — Should the answer of any intermediate number be demanded, as 37 for example, the question denoting 30 would be asked thus:

What Number of, &c.?   *Please to count them?*

What Number denotes 30, and the remark, "*please to count,*" signifies that there were more than five more in contemplation. Thus, the subject imagines 30, and commences to count thus, 1, 2, RING. We now have by this process 32 and the 5 additional, as 32 –|– 5 are 37.

LESSON IV.

What *do I hold* in my hand ?   A pair of gloves.

Are they *ladies'* or gentlemen's gloves ?   LADIES' gloves.

Now reverse the question thus :

Are they *gentlemen's* or ladies' gloves ?   Gentlemen's gloves.   (See example for color.)

What kind of an *instrument* is this ?   A pocket-knife.   (See color of handle, &c.)

What number of blades ?   One.

What *is the* number of blades ?   Two.

What number can *you see* ?   Three.

What number *can you tell* ?   Four.   If more than five, refer to the table of Numerals.

Here's a *rare article*, what is it ?   A handkerchief.

What color ?   White.

What quality? Linen.

What *is the* quality ? Cotton.

Can you tell me the quality ? Silk.

Describe the quality of this or that ? Cloth. (See color.)

What *is this?* A porte-monnaie or pocket-book. (Repeat.)

"A porte-monnaie" or pocket-book ; but which of the two is it ? A porte-monnaie. (Reverse as in gloves.)

What is this I hold in my hand ? A watch.

What quality? Silver.

Can you tell me the quality ? It has the appearance of gold.

Answer the question *direct?* I would take it for gold.

Can you tell me the quality ? It has the *appearance* of gold.

"Appearance" of gold ; what do you mean by that ? I mean, it's a poor example for genuine, like the owner.

What have I in my hand ? A hat. (See color.)

What kind of a *Fancy article* is this ? A snuff or tobacco-box ? (Reverse as in porte-monnaie, gloves, &c.)

What does this instrument *pertain* to ? To music.

Here is a very *curious* instrument, what is it ? A lancet.

Describe the *nature* of the *article* I hold in my hand ? An opera-glass.

If you can *discriminate* an article through the *back*

of your *head*, tell me what this is? An umbrella. (See color, &c.)

Here, what *do you* call this? A cap. (See color.)

Here, *what's* this? A cigar.

Here, *what's* this *for?* A cigar-case. (Repeat.)
A case? A cigar-holder.

What *kind* of an *article* is this? A cane. (See color.)

Here is a *common* article, what is it? A tumbler.

Here is *something else!* A stick of some kind.

Do you know what this is? A toothpick.

What quality? Ivory.

What quality, *direct?* Silver.

What *kind?* Goose-quill.

Can you tell the *quality direct?* Gold.

Here is an article of *great value*, what is it? A pair of spectacles. (See quality, &c.)

The gentleman *desires* you to name this article? A boot.

The gentleman is *anxious* you tell what this is? A shoe.

I believe I am *puzzled* to know what this is, can you tell? Curiosity (curiosity), spoken with surprise; but it is a greater curiosity for me to see and not know what you know and don't see.

This article the owner *prefers* to keep? A comb. If but one comb, answer instantly (correct); if it should be a pair of combs, make a slight pause between the word comb and the word correct.

Here is *an article used by ladies*, what is it? A pencil. (See color and quality.)

What is this article *used for?* Soap

What are *these?* A pair of scissors.

Tell me what this is? India-rubber.

Please to tell me what these are? A pair of tweezers.

Will you tell me what this is? A pocket-slate.

Here's a lady's *favorite* article, what is it? A ring. (See quality.)

What does this *gentleman hold in his hand?* A musical instrument.

What does this *lady hold in her hand?* A bonnet.

This is of some *importance,* what is it? A penny.

Here is an *exceeding* common article, what is it? A book. Correct. Should the word *a book* be repeated, it signifies a blank book. (See comb, for example.)

What *kind* of a book? A map.

Name this? A nail.

Hand me *some other article;* but never mind—A screw.

A screw? A corkscrew.

What do you *see* in my hand? A bottle.

What does this *box contain, or for?* A matchbox.

What *kind* of a box is this? A cap-box.

What quality of box is this? A fancy or toilet-box

What *kind of money* or coin is this? It is no money.

What is it then? A medal.

What is this *glass for?* An eye-glass.

A *gent's favorite* article? A watch-guard.

Repeat a watch-guard? A watch-chain. (See quality.)

What does this *belong to?* A watch.

What part? The seal. (See quality.)

What part of *apparel* is this? A lady's shawl.

Name this for the lady or gent, as the case may be? A ribbon.

TELL the *lady* or *gent* what this is? Lace.

What do *ladies use this* for? Thread.

Can you tell what this is? A key. (Remark.) A key? A safe-key.

What *is this* key USED for? A door-key.

When is *this* key used? At night, or night-key.

What do you *think* it is used for ?   A trunk-key.

What *use* does the *owner* make of it ?   A watch-key.

What quality of key ?   Iron.

Can you tell me the quality ?   Brass.

Can you tell me the quality *direct ?.*   Gold.

Can you tell me what *these* are ?   A bunch of keys.

Count the number ?   1, 2, 3, 4, 5.   (If more than five, then resort to the bell as before.)

Here's an article—I *scarcely* know what it is my-self?   A stone.   (Remark.)   A stone ?   A marble.

What color ?   White.

What is it used for ?   Chalk.

What color is *this* stone, and what is it used for ?
Red chalk.

This is something of *vast importance* to every man, what is it ?   A piece of money or coin.

What quality ?   Silver.

What value ?   Three cents.

How much value ?   Five cents.

How much *is the* value ?   Six and a quarter cents.

How much is *it worth ?*   Ten cents.

What value is this coin ?   Twenty-five cents.

What is it worth ?   Fifty cents.

What is this *coin worth ?*   One dollar.

This is something of vast importance, &c.

Can you tell me the quality *direct ?*   Gold coin.

What value ?   One dollar·

How much value ?   Two dollars and fifty cents.

How much *is the* value ?   Three dollars.

Of how much is the value ?   Five dollars.

What is this *coin worth ?*   Ten dollars.

What is the *extreme* value of this coin ?   Twenty dollars.

What *two figures* denote its value ?   Fifty dollars.

What kind of a *book* is this, or the gentleman has just handed me a *valuable book*, &c. ?   It is no book.

What is it then ?   A bank note.

What value ?   One dollar.

How much value ?   Two dollars.

How much *is the value ?*   Three dollars.

How much *is it worth ?*   Four dollars.

OF HOW MUCH *is the value ?*   Five dollars.

How much is this *note worth ?*   Ten dollars.

What is the *extreme* value of *this note ?*   Twenty dollars.

What *two figures* denote its denomination ?   Fifty dollars.

What *three* figures denote its denomination ?   One hundred dollars.

What state ?   The present state.

What city or town ?   The present.

What day ?   What week ?   What time ?   What date, &c. ?   Always the present subject then in view.

EXAMPLE.

What day did he or she go ?   To-day.

What year ?   1855, &c.

The following examples are calculated to denote within fifteen minutes of any required time.

From these examples we find but two hours specified by the questions.   And it is expected that every subject, when about to perform this experiment, can certainly judge within two hours of the correct time.

Thus he can apply the following rule at any time, day or night.   Should the hands of the watch or clock be at great variance with the correct time, you may then refer to the numeral table to find out the figures denoting such time.   Then add this rule, and you cannot fail to arrive at the correct time denoted by such watch, let it be right or wrong,

What time is it by this watch ?   (Ring.)   Eight o'clock exactly, or one hour before the time designed to be answered.

What time is it now ?   (Ring.)   Fifteen minutes after eight.

What time at present ?   (Ring.)   Half-past eight.

Can you tell the time ? (Ring.) Fifteen minutes to nine o'clock.

What time is it by this watch ? Nine o'clock. (The exact intermediate time designed to be answered.)

What time is it now ? Fifteen minutes after nine.

What time at present ? Half-past nine.

Can you tell the time? Fifteen minutes to ten o'clock.

What is the exact time ? Ten o'clock.

BELL QUESTIONS.

Bell questions are voluntary terms made use of, and not being a direct question put to the subject ; but the remark made to terminate by one stroke of the bell. By this process it seems that the bell is the only medium by which the intelligence is given ; thus it always confounds the mind of the spectator, how that, by the same one direct and only sound of the signal-bell, could give sufficient intelligence for the explanation of the color and quality of a difficult article (say the entire description of a watch, and time likewise.) In order to make this appear plain, I have annexed a few examples. Thus, addressing the persons present :

Subjects are enabled by this process to see as it were any article in *posession* of another. Ring. A lady's muff.

Some very *industrious* person must have brought this article. Ring. A thimble.

I *will pass* this article out of my hand into that of *yours, sir.* Ring. A money-purse.

It does seem a *mystery* even to me to see and know how this trick is accomplished. Ring. A miniature.

Many persons would be easily convinced that this was actually *clairvoyance,* but we repeat this is a trick forever. Ring. A lady's veil.

This trick is well calculated to confound the minds of many *intelligent men.* Ring. A letter.

This trick is *susceptible* of being carried to a greater *perfection* than this. Ring. A card.

We make many *mistakes* but seldom *detected.* Ring. A necklace or pertaining to the neck.

I wonder if the subject *foresees* the articles *held* up. Ring. A garment.

We admit of this as being a trick only, yet a very *novel one too.* Ring. A paper. Ring. A news-paper.

This principle so frequently manifested, I was a going to say by gentlemen, but never mind. Ring. A rule. Ring. A tape line or rule.

Ah ! this is *handsome enough.* Ring. A breastpin.

The *subject sees these* articles as *readily* as you do. Ring. A looking-glass.

A toy may be known by one full stroke of the bell, during a short interval, say five seconds, or thereabouts.

An arnament may be known by a half condensed stroke of the bell, by making one stroke and immediately touching the bell with the ends of the fingers, stopping off the sound.

Inclose this article in your hand. Ring. A buckle. This is a *precious* good trick, yet there are but few who can carry it out successfully. Ring. A lock of hair.

Young man, hold that in your hand. There's a button for you.

It matters not what the articles are, but all will be readily *described alike.* Ring. A check. Repeat a check. A pass check.

What is this check used for ? A baggage check.

Produce any article you please for description. Ring. A keepsake.

This is a——(interrupted by a—). Ring. A lady's reticule.

It is surprising to see how articles are described so accurately. Ring. Sealing wax.

I thank you for that. Ring. A piece of candy.

꠸ ꠸ꠞ ꠞ this is pretty good, I guess I'll keep it. Ring. ꠞry.

‒‒‒‒ꠋ of this would be agreeable. Ring. Fruit.

Have you any more of the same sort? Ring. Pass that spice over this way.

Well! well! what next will people hand up? Ring. A file.

Communications in this science are simple enough for any one to acquire in a short time. Ring. A brush. (Correct.) *repeat a brush!* A tooth brush.

It BECOMES very *difficult* to describe articles, particularly if we do not know what they are. Ring. Dental or surgical instrument.

Which is it, the first or last named instrument? The first, or a dental instrument. (Reverse for the opposite.)

I PRESUME he or she can tell what it is. Ring. Needles. (*repeat ring.*) Pins.

BELL EXERCISES

Are only repeated strokes of the bell denoting the time when the articles are held up without using any language as a corresponding medium. (See example.)

Ring. 1. A pair of gloves.
" 2. A handkerchief.
" 3. A hat.
" 4. A black hat.
" 5. A cap.
" 6. A black cap.
" 7. A lady.
" 8. A lady's hand
" 9. A lady's bonnet.
" 10. A garment.
" 11. A nose.
" 12. A rumsucker's nose (changing to another)
" 13. He professes to be a gentleman.
" 14. Deeply in love.

" 15. With ladies and whiskey.
" 16. Shall I count the ladies he loves ?
" 17. (*This ring denotes yes.*)
" 18. 1. 2. 3. 4. 5. 6. 7. 8. 9. 10. 11. 12. 13. 14.
15. 16. 17. 18. 19. 20. (*Interrupted.*) Hold on ! hold on!

Why does he love so many ?   He follows your example.

What example ?   To fall in love with all he meets, whether they be white or black.

That will do, I perceive you know it all.

Note.—The operator during these exercises should be very careful to know that he can procure the above list of articles, or at least a similar list which he can arrange at any time with his subject; and you can change your list each evening at pleasure, and not be confined exclusively to the above memoranda.

Note.—The following examples will correctly denote any century or date, from 1854 back to 1400.   Articles or coin dated further back than this will seldom if ever be offered for explanation.

EXAMPLE.

What date is this coin or article, &c. ?   1800.
Of what date, &c. ?   1700.
Tell the date, &c. ?   1600.
Can you tell the date, &c. ?   1500.
Describe the date, &c. ?   1400.

Two special questions will be given to denote 1853 and 54, as so many articles are presented having one of the above dates.

What date is this ?   1854.
What date DO YOU *see ?*   1853.

In order to ascertain any intermediate date, as 1804 for example.

WHAT DATE, or *What number can you tell ?*   1804.

See the first example on page 54, "*what date ;*" by this we have 18 or 1800.   "What number can you tell ? " (see page 49), we have 4 or 04 ;   thus 18—04 or 1804.   Suppose the number to be answered was 1710.

"*Of what date ? Please count.*"   1700—1, 5, 3, 4, 5, (Ring). 6, 7, 8, 9, 10—1710.

Thus we have at once 1700 and 10 or 1710.

In these examples it will be well to get a perfect knowledge of the tables of Numerals, and particularly the exercises of the bell.

Now suppose the date to be 1830.   Example.

What date or number ?   Ring.   1830.

What date ?   1800.

What number ?   Ring.   30.   Thus we have 1830— a repeated stroke of the bell denotes five above as usual. Thus 1830.   Ring.   1835, and all other numbers to be calculated in the same manner.

In no case must the subject name the century until he has first ascertained the additional number of years, as in 1710, "of what date," must be borne in mind until the remaining numbers be calculated, thus answering two questions at once. "*Of what date ?*" "*Please count?*"   Thus 1710. *

Ring A, B.

"   A, B, C, D, E, F, G, H, I, J, K, L, M, N, O.

"   A, B, C, D, E, F, G, H, I, J, K, L, M, N, O.

"   A, B, C, D, E, F, G, H, I, J, K.   Ring.   Thus we have spelled out the word book—and any correspondence can be conducted in the very same manner.

A list of articles generally presented by the audience for description :

Hats, Caps, Gloves, Canes, Watches and Chains, Keys, Pencils, Rings, Books, Coins, Bank notes, Medals, Snuff boxes, Tobacco boxes, Match boxes, Cap boxes, Fancy boxes, Strings, Sticks, Stones, Paper, Letters, Combs, Handkerchiefs, Breast pins, Pocket knives, Screws, Nails, Tooth brushes, Dental instruments, Surgical instruments, Musical instruments, Maps, Shawls, Cards, Cravats, Pens, Thimbles, Brushes, Buttons, Mirrors, Garments, Ribbons, Tape, Laces,

---

* It was impossible to give the correct dates without first uniting two distinct questions by the word "or," thus making them appear but one question.

Cord, Scissors, Thread, Needles, Pins, Muffs, Spectacles, Cases, Cigars, Purses, Veils, Watch guards, Ladies' reticules, Tuning forks, Pocket slates, Pass checks, Sealing wax, Tape lines, Locks of hair, Opera glasses, Eye glasses, Lancets, Keepsakes, Umbrellas, Buckles, Files, Bottles, Perfumery, Candy, Fruit, Spices, Toys, Miniatures, Boots, Shoes, Tumblers, Cloth, India-rubber, Soap.

Names or articles can be spelled out in the very same way alphabetically. (Example.)

CONCLUSION.

We now have had a brief illustration of the mysteries of "Second Sight," or the pretended art of seeing without eyes. You have, I hope, found it to be a pleasant and interesting study; and should you wish to introduce the experiments before an audience or private party, bring your subject before the visitors; now take a pocket handkerchief and fold it up and place it over the eyes of the subject, with face first to the company; then make a few polite remarks respecting the trick as not being clairvoyance, mesmerism, ventriloquism, or any other of the popular illusions of the day.

Now procure some of the articles contained in the list; after a few have been named, remark to the company that you believe the subject can see through the handkerchief; and you will please the company better by turning your back to them and then describe the articles held up; or should there be an adjoining room convenient, place your subject in that, under such circumstances, however, that they are enabled to hear every *sound that is uttered distinctly.*

N. B.—Should any articles be presented in the course of your experiments not contained in the list, you must then prepare yourself with some new cue in the list; in this way you will soon be able to swell up the catalogue to a wonderful size, by writing all your new questions down on paper and committing them to memory as the others.

www.ingramcontent.com/pod-product-compliance
Lightning Source LLC
Chambersburg PA
CBHW020029030726

47499CB00007B/2335